LAKELAND DOCTOR

D1492937

Hilary sometimes wondered why she stuck to her job as Doctor Blake Kinross's secretary-receptionist. He was too demanding, took her too much for granted. It was only when an old flame of Blake's arrived in their quiet Lakeland village that Hilary understood her own heart . . .

LAKELAND DOCTOR

BY

JEAN CURTIS

MILLS & BOON LIMITED
London · Sydney · Toronto

First published in Great Britain 1972
by Mills & Boon Limited, 17–19 Foley Street,
London W1A 1DR

This edition 1980

ISBN 0 263 73245 2

Filmset in 10 on 11½pt Baskerville

Made and printed in Great Britain by
C. Nicholls & Company Ltd.,
The Philips Park Press, Manchester

CHAPTER ONE

SPRING had come with more than usual reluctance to Lakeland this year. But now, on a day of deepening gold sunlight, Hilary Talgarth stood before the door of the statesman's house which, built just after 1600, had seen many generations of her family born and die within its sturdy walls. She was watching the young lambs skipping on the hillsides, safe now from iron night frosts beside their placid mothers, and drawing in a deep breath of the keen, still cold air, felt that life was wakening to new hope with April's swifter coming of spring.

A year and a half ago all had been shadowed with the darkness of her father's death; but merciful time had gradually replaced grief with tranquil remembrance, and the busy days that filled her life were helped by the knowledge that her elder and only brother now tilled the soil and ran Willowbeck Farm and its men with a sure and steady hand: which meant that where Talgarths had been the first in Elizabeth Tudor's day Talgarths would, God willing, still go on into the uncertain later years of the twentieth century.

Hilary herself had quite another job; one strange to her family yet which she had willingly accepted. For a brief year she had trained in a big teaching hospital, but her health had not allowed her to follow the greatest wish of her life – to become a nurse. She had had to return to Tarnmere, but all she had learned in her absence had luckily not been lost. The village doctor, old Doctor James Kendrick, known affectionately to all for miles around as "our Dr. Jim", had very peacefully departed from his lifelong devotion to his patients at the age of eighty-five, spry, alert and clever to the last; and a younger man had taken his place. A man with a difficult job, so the elders of the village prophesied, and they were right.

Young Dr. Blake Kinross had not found the first year of his practice easy: a fact which no one would have guessed from his calm and perhaps slightly forbidding exterior. Tall, brown-haired and very good-looking in a rugged way, but with a forthright and sometimes caustic manner that did not by any means endear him to everyone, his skill had gradually won him reluctant and then admiring adherents; though some still stood out and lamented that: "T'old doctor's ways were more to our ways of thinking, I reckon! But there, times move and folks change, so there's nowt to be done about it!"

But for Hilary, though she had missed dear "Dr. Jim" almost as much as her own father, the advent of a new medico to Tarnmere proved an unexpected blessing. For the new doctor had desperately needed a secretary-receptionist with nursing experience, and in the girl who had been so heartbroken when her health had forced her to give up full-time nursing, he had found what he wanted.

But though Hilary found a job which suited her, she had also found an employer who could be on occasion both difficult and infuriating.

Yet on this day of spring sunshine that bathed the further horizon in a shimmering blue haze through which loomed the shadowy peaks of the mighty mountains of Cumberland in distant and austere beauty, Hilary could only feel at peace – not just with her employer, but with the whole world. Tarnmere valley was surrounded by smaller, kindlier hills whose lower slopes were scattered with pine and larch and hawthorn. Those other, greater mountains, Helvellyn, Cat-bells, Blencathra were little more than a far-off whisper framing fells of a harsher beauty which, glimpsed from the paths far above Willow-beck Farm, could be seen to merge like the blue waves of a rocky sea into the breathtaking grandeur of the Scottish Border.

Hilary preferred the nearer, homelier signs of spring; the golden celandines above the rushing icy waters of the beck that tumbled over sunlit stones beneath the moss-grown bridge where yellow wagtails conducted their first tentative courtship under the nodding branches of wild plum and cherry blossom putting forth their first tentative buds in the April sunlight.

"Hilary love, were you thinking of going into the village? Because I'm running short of sugar and flour, and there'll be extra baking with Tim's birthday on Friday."

She turned quickly at the sound of the voice behind her, her amber eyes lighting to sudden laughter as she looked across at the buxom figure of her cousin Priscilla. Mrs. Brathay had looked after the domestic side of Willowbeck Farm ever since the death of Hilary's mother. Widowed herself, she had turned up when the Talgarth's were all dazed by the sudden tragedy that had overtaken them; and it was thanks to her brisk but kindly management that John Talgarth's last years had been made as comfortable as they were. Cousin Priscilla was still apt to treat Hilary and Tim as the children they had been on her arrival. Nothing ever disturbed her placid confidence, and both Hilary and her brother loved her dearly – not only for the tower of strength she had been to their father, but for the never-failing affection she gave to themselves.

"Dear Cousin Priscilla, you seem to forget Tim is twenty-five this year," his sister observed. "You don't need to bother any longer—"

"Now try to tell me there's the man living who hasn't a sweet tooth," Cousin Priscilla retorted. "If there's not a currant pasty as well as an apple one – and my best plum cake besides – he'd feel reet neglected! Didn't my own Harry – and a sad rip he could be, though I loved him dearly – always say to me 'Pris, if I get to heaven and you're not there to cook for me, I'll go straight down and sign up with old Nick'!"

"And who would blame him?" Hilary agreed. "But *not* very complimentary to expect to find you in the other place!"

"Ah!" Mrs. Brathay, her plump face wreathed in smiles, shook an admonishing finger. "By the way, who do you think was full of compliments for my cooking when he called the other day? No less than Dr. Kinross himself! When I gave him a cup of tea and some cake and currant pasty, he actually vowed his old housekeeper Nanny Tyson still had something to learn!"

"Such treachery!" Hilary's eyes danced. "Mrs. Tyson will be horribly jealous if she ever hears of that!"

"Not she!" Cousin Priscilla shook her head. "She'd just say he was being polite! . . . But for all he may not be our dear Dr. James, that young man has the root of the matter in him where Tarnmere is concerned. A reet fine lad and a very good doctor when all's said and done; and you'll find nine out of ten in the village agree with me, Hilary dear."

"Yes, he's born to the job," Hilary replied, knowing rather to her annoyance that for some unknown reason her colour had deepened. "Is there anything else I can get you at Mr. Hardisty's while I'm about it?"

After a moment's thought Mrs. Brathay announced that she was short of crystallised cherries; and a few minutes later, a scarf tied over her red-gold hair, Hilary was walking down the winding road, over the bridge that spanned Applegarth Beck as if flowed beneath fern and moss-covered rocks towards the lake.

"A very good doctor." Pausing on the bridge to watch a pair of moorhens busy looking for nest materials among the stones bordering the swirling water, Hilary found those words echoing in her ears. Well, so he was; and if he could be sometimes an impatient and exasperating person to

work for, one certainly did not think the worse of him for that, however irritated he might make one at times.

And of course Cousin Priscilla, for all her sixty grey-haired years, had as soft a spot as the rest of her sex for those tall, rugged good looks and – when he chose – extremely charming manner. Not only the elderly succumbed to that sudden three-cornered smile which could make its possessor change from a slightly remote person to someone warm and delightful, his younger female patients were even more ready to do so. At the same time the doctor was liked by his own sex, and certainly could not be labelled "a ladies' man."

Resuming her walk, her rather unwanted reflections concerning her employer were agreeably broken as she caught sight of a small, slight, dark-haired figure standing at the top of a sloping meadow, intent before an easel; a splash of colour herself in blue slacks and a scarlet shirt under her painting smock.

Looking up, Hilary smiled to herself, but knew better than to shout a greeting. When Veronica Frant, known to all her friends as "Frant" – because as she rightly said "Veronica" simply wasn't her! – was painting, those friends knew better than to interrupt that extremely eminent and brilliant young painter's work – which was more than could be said for many visitors, or certain neighbours with more curiosity than good manners. Those pausing to comment or try to start a conversation about whatever subject might be on the canvas were apt to be shrivelled either by icy politeness, or a sudden scorching request to be left alone: an experience that had caused more than one interloper to feel singed.

Watching the distant figure of her best friend Hilary smiled again. Dear Frant! So brilliant and so unassuming about the work which was her life, and which had gained for her fame both in England and abroad. To own "a Frant" was to proclaim oneself a person of both money and good taste, or sometimes merely of the former – the two all too often not going together. Tarnmere, in the county of her birth, saw her for large parts of the year in the small house with the big studio overlooking the lake. Sometimes pupils were taken at quite staggering fees; but more often Frant worked there alone, as she was doing this season.

The slight figure stepped back from the easel and contemplated it a moment; then turning, caught sight of Hilary on the road below. Hilary waved and would have passed on, but her friend waved back, shouting:

"Oi! Come up a minute. I want you."

"O.K." Hilary crossed to where steps set in the drystone wall formed a rough stile and swung herself over. As she climbed the slope she was greeted by Frant's rather elfish grin.

"Being ever so tactful, weren't you?" she commented. "But I'm finished for now, and require a cigarette and a natter. I've been at the damn thing for nearly two hours."

Hilary looked at the canvas – a startling and yet tranquil study of mountains and the eastern end of the lake, a sapphire half oval lit by morning sunshine – and the artist added warningly:

"I'm not through with it yet. So don't say a word!"

"I wasn't going to," Hilary assured her, and accepted a cigarette.

"I know you weren't. That, Hilary my sweet, is why I bear with you – among other things." Frant lit her own cigarette and gave the canvas a hard, impersonal stare before turning away to replace tubes and brushes in a large box of quite remarkable untidiness. "Did I tell you about the other evening up at Blemere Tarn? I thought at that time of day, with the season too early for dratted tourists and autograph-hunters, I could be sure of peace. But no, that old horror Gilbert Downing appeared like

10

some **ghastly** elemental, bumbling forward and fluting: 'Hard at work so late? May I be *terribly* rude and just take a *wee* peep! Such a glorious purple light above the water, is there not?' "

Hilary laughed. "Did you slay him with a look?"

"Take more than a look to kill that one, unfortunately. I said 'There isn't a purple light!' between my teeth, just like that. And he said, 'Oh? I defer to genius, but I thought there was just a *wee* tinge of purple.' And went on and on until I could willingly have thrown him into the tarn. Of course by the time he raised his horrible green hat and doddered away, the light I wanted had gone – greenish-blue and *not* in the least purple, blast him!"

"Poor Frant," Hilary sympathised. "It's odd that such a large man should work so hard at what he calls 'my art' and produce such limp pictures."

"Limp!" her friend exploded. "He spends days on twee little water-colours that would disgrace a fourth form art class. Thrashing about before his easel like a mad walrus—"

"Why walrus?" asked Hilary mildly.

Frant thrust her beautiful hands into her disgraceful painting smock. "Well – that moustache, for one thing." She laughed suddenly. "You'll say I'm an idiot to get so irritated, but his sudden appearances are the bane of my life. Anyway, this morning hasn't been so bad. Where are you off to?"

Hilary told her, and Frant lifted the canvas off its easel. "I'll come with you and when you've done your bit of shopping we can go on to my place and have some tea," she said. "This is dry enough to handle carefully now – perhaps you'd like to take the box."

"Of course. I'd love a cup of tea, but I mustn't stay long. I've got to call in at the surgery and put in an hour's typing – I'm a bit behind and I don't want to leave it all until tomorrow morning."

"But surely this is your afternoon off?" Frant demanded, glancing at her with one dark eyebrow raised.

Hilary laughed, colouring slightly. "Yes, of course it is. But I often look in for an hour on a Wednesday evening – otherwise there's so much to do the next day."

"H'm. You certainly do work for your living," her friend commented rather drily. "And of course Blake Kinross takes it all completely for granted, I'll be bound."

"Well, naturally – when does he ever spare himself?" Hilary sounded a little defensive, quite forgetting how her employer's undoubtedly casual acceptance of her hard work was sometimes apt to irritate her.

"True enough," Frant agreed. "But that doesn't mean you have to go at the same headlong pace. Does he ever remember that you're supposed still not to take too much out of yourself? After all, it's less than a year since you had to leave St. Winifred's."

"Oh, I'm fit enough now – for my present job anyway." Hilary sighed, and a shadow passed over her face at the mention of the great teaching hospital she had been forced to leave, having worked to breaking point. "If I hadn't plenty of work I'd go crazy in a month." She laughed suddenly. "Odd, when you think what a long line of farming stock I come from, that the idea of such a life fills me with dismay! Tim says I'm an unnatural freak and a blot on the Talgarth family! But luckily he understands, bless him."

"He's a very understanding person," Frant agreed. "But of course one of these days he'll be marrying and carrying on the family. Ever thought what you'll do then?"

"Oh, I'll cross that stile when I come to it." Hilary's tone sounded lighter than she felt. "I like my present work, so I don't think I'd ever look back. Or go back, for that matter, to any city. Too noisy and hectic."

"I should think Dr. Kinross would have something to

say if you ever tried to leave," Frant remarked, carefully changing the canvas she was carrying from her left to her right hand.

"Good heavens, why should he? I could be replaced easily enough." Hilary's tone was casual, but her friend did not fail to note her quick, slightly startled look.

Frant gave her soft, very attractive laugh. "Don't be daft, lovey! Of course you couldn't be easily replaced. How many young women are there with nursing experience, ready to come and do arduous secretarial work in a village like this? They either want the bright lights, or if they come into the country it's because they wish to go truly rural and marry a farmer! Blake Kinross would be livid if you even suggested going elsewhere."

"Well, I'm not thinking of doing so at the moment, so the question doesn't arise," Hilary said serenely. "I'd better get the sugar and flour now – Mr. Hardisty will be shut by the time I come back."

They had reached the foot of the hill, having passed several cottages and a stretch of wall belonging to one of the bigger houses where a belt of woodland, burgeoning into pale green, screened all but purple-grey slate roofs and round Westmorland chimneys from the passer-by.

Emerging into the village square with its old coaching inn standing back in its gardens where the archway to the yard was a constant object of tourists' cameras, a bookshop and stationers showed a window of surprisingly varied contents away to the right; ahead lay the chief grocers of the village, and next to it the post office.

Further along the road leading to the lake rose the squat square tower of the Norman church outlined against its background of giant elms, and beside it the long white building of the vicarage stood at the top of a slight rise amid its charming gardens which just now were golden with daffodils and early narcissi, picked out by the purple

13

of crocus and blue of scilla flowers, while a celandine-bordered stream ran below the burgeoning hawthorn and hazel hedge.

"I'll only be a few minutes – you go on and I'll catch you up." Hilary pushed open the door into Mr. Hardisty's rather dark little shop which, for all its packets of detergents and breakfast cereals with horrible free gifts "as shown on TV", yet had a delightfully aromatic scent of brown sugar, spices, dried fruit and herbs which would have been instantly familiar to the great-grandparents of the villagers who were his customers. Mr. Hardisty was, as he only too often liked to proclaim, "rising seventy-five", and still took pride in serving dry goods in blue paper bags folded into stiff cones, and sported over his mustard tweed trousers an enormous apron whose spotless white matched his silvery moustache. His very blue eyes under their shaggy brows had lost little of their colour with the passing years.

"Six pounds of sugar and four of flour, Miss Hilary. And some candied cherries? That'll be Mrs. Brathay wanting them for Mr. Tim's birthday, no doubt," the old grocer observed. "Let's see – he's twenty-five come next Thursday – and it seems only yesterday he was a five-year-old coming in here with your pretty mother, and being given a lump of brown sugar or a piece of candied peel."

"That lovely peel with all the sugar in it!" Hilary sighed. "It seems almost to have vanished nowadays."

"Like so much else that's good," Mr. Hardisty returned. "Lots of smart packaging and precious little flavour – as with groceries, so 'tis with modern life! My grandchildren say I'm an old moaner, and in some ways so I am. But when they tell me you can't put back the clock I answer that's something I'm only too well aware of. Of course," he added, "some things were worse for the poor, and yet most of 'em still managed to enjoy themselves

14

sometimes – all the more for not having so many holidays as they have now. But there was quality to things when I was young – aye, and to folk too!"

Hilary smiled placatingly, then as another customer entered the shop, she bade him good-day and made her escape, rather thankful to avoid a further airing of what was generally known in the village as "Old Hardisty's Hobby-horse".

Quickening her steps, she turned a corner to find Frant leaning against the low wall that stretched in front of the gardens of one of the smaller private hotels, gazing across the valley to where the high peak known as Yeatholm Crag raised its rocky summit against the pale blue sky in austere beauty. Its wooded lower slopes stretched down to the far side of the lake whose waters glimmered like a sapphire set round with emerald; distant cattle like Noah's Ark figures grazed in the brilliant green fields, and on a landing stage beside a boathouse gaily-shirted holidaymakers made an added splash of colour.

Drawing on her cigarette, her canvas carefully propped beside her, Frant looked round with a smile.

"You've been a long time buying a few pounds of sugar and flour," she observed. "Old Hardisty philosophising again?"

"Yes, but luckily I got away," Hilary replied. And as they continued on their way: "Hullo! What's John's latest acquisition, I wonder?"

"John's latest—?" Frant looked up quickly, and then glancing ahead to where before what had been a pair of cottages but was now half a dwelling and half a shop with a long window over which a board painted in black letters on a white background proclaimed "John Dallam. Antiques", a rather battered estate car was drawn up, and a large young man in a check shirt and corduroys was endeavouring to pull something that was obviously extra heavy out from between the doors of the vehicle.

15

"Hoy!" Frant shouted. "What are you up to, may I ask?"

There was a loud bang and a regrettable word, then the owner of the estate car emerged, nursing a thumb. He was a very large young man indeed, tall and broad-shouldered, with a shock of flaming red hair above a pleasantly ugly face with a square jaw, a humorous mouth and the freckles that go with fiery colouring.

"Sorry for the language, but you shouldn't frighten a fellow," he apologised. "Frant, my lovely, how sweet of you to be interested in my sordid trade. It's a corner cupboard from that cottage they've just pulled down up on Scardale Bank, blast them for the philistines they are. How I hate property developers."

"Amen to that," Frant agreed. "But I am not lovely, nor, may I remind you, am I yours!"

"Worse luck!" John Dallam's smile was a very charming one, and made him almost good-looking. "But that can soon be mended. Will you marry me?"

"No, I won't," said Frant serenely. "And well you know it – or ought to by now."

"I do like a girl who knows her own mind. But I'd like it even better if she knew when to change it." John Dallam drew out a rather disgraceful pipe and proceeded to fill it while he grinned at Hilary, "Let me get this thing into the shop and put the bus away, then you two girls come in and have some tea. Poor bachelor fare, but I can't help that when I'm treated with such unkindness."

Hilary laughed. "That's a whopper!" she remarked. "Your Mrs. Dalgarth looks after you every bit as well as Cousin Priscilla does Tim and myself."

"Quite true," Frant agreed. "But he's always being sorry for himself, this lad. And here, if I mistake not, Watson, come some potential customers, so you can't litter your premises with females during working hours.

16

Hilary is coming to tea with me – but if you like to look in, in half an hour you can have some too."

"I will if I can," John Dallam promised. "What it is to be a poor working man and not one's own master, let alone a gent of leisure. And I bet they don't buy anything," he added, lowering his voice as a mixed party of elderly and young tourists approached. "Ten to one they only want some advice as to how much Great-Aunt Gertrude's tea-set is worth—"

He waved a cheery hand and turned towards the shop, while the two girls went on up the road.

CHAPTER TWO

THERE was a fairly lengthy silence. As they approached Frant's neat little white house on the lakeshore, with its gardens sloping down to the water, Hilary gave her friend a sidelong glance.

"What a dear John is," she remarked. "Although he's only been here three years and used to be known as 'that young chap from Carlisle way', he's been quite accepted. Everyone likes him."

"Do they?" Frant asked a little absently. "Yes, I suppose they do. He is rather a sweetie."

"And he is very much in love with you," Hilary told her.

"Is he?"

"Oh, my dear Frant! You're neither blind nor stupid." Hilary gave an exasperated sigh. "I've an idea that you're making the poor boy very unhappy behind that cheerful façade he puts up."

"Nonsense!" Frant said defensively. "He's simply got into the way of thinking himself in love with me, that's all. His proposals have just become rather a joke—"

"Not to him." Hilary shook her head. "It isn't my business, so you're perfectly entitled to snub me if you choose, but I've sometimes an idea that where he's concerned you're not so entirely without heart as you make out."

Frant stared ahead at her garden gate, a little half smile touching her generous mouth. "Maybe I'm not," she admitted. "But I have no intention of getting married – anyway, for some time yet. And by the time I do, no doubt John will have fallen for some nice domestic girl who'll give him the sort of home he needs. Now I'm not domestic,

18

and never could be. Also, there's my work, and without wanting to make a song and dance about it, it *is* of some importance. John is thrilled with it at present, but I've an idea that if he were married to it he would see things in quite a different light."

"Meaning that he might resent it? I don't think so," Hilary told her. "He's got too much sense of humour and generosity to mind if people pointed him out as 'Frant's husband'."

"Maybe." Frant shrugged her shoulders, and then seeing the reproach in her friend's eyes, smiled rather wryly. "You think I'm being unkind, but it might be less kind to give in to John. You'll have to give this particular pot more time to simmer, lovey."

"O.K., I won't come the matchmaking girl-friend," Hilary promised, and they both laughed.

A few minutes later they were in Frant's charming blue and yellow sitting-room overlooking the lake from long bow-fronted windows. It was sparsely, almost severely furnished, yet everything was in perfect harmony in a manner reminiscent of the exquisite civilisation that had once been China. The furnishings were unobtrusively modern; a very beautiful silk-washed carpet in dusty pink and subdued turquoise set off the ebony-wood chairs and long low table of gilt and rose marble to perfection. A single covered yellow vase of the Ming period on a stand of carved rosewood stood beside the fireplace, and on the mantelpiece two horses in rose quartz and the tranquil figure of a K'wan Yin in white jade dwelt in aloof beauty. Against one wall was a black and gold lacquer cabinet inlaid with mother-o'-pearl, above which an eighteenth-century painting on silk of a summer pavilion with ladies and gentlemen of the Peking court glowed jewel-like in the afternoon light. And on the opposite wall was an unexpected bureau-bookcase packed with volumes that gave an informal yet in no way incongruous air of slightly

19

untidy homeliness to what might have been too formal a room for the country. But Frant had her own kind of genius for making a home, and though her own sanctum was a cheerfully untidy place for unashamedly dropping ash and putting down cups and saucers or glasses without fear of spoiling anything, this tranquil room was a favourite with her friends and an object of admiration to visitors.

Crossing to the long windows, she threw them open and stepped out on to the small paved terrace beyond.

"We'll have tea here," she announced. "It's warm and sheltered in the sun, with no midges at this time of the year."

"Lovely!" Hilary followed her out and sank down in one of the wicker cushioned chairs with a contented sigh. "But do tell Mrs. Elleray that a cup of tea and some bread and butter are all that's necessary. Otherwise I know she'll serve up something quite as ruinous to the figure as Cousin Priscilla does."

"Useless," Frant returned, her eyes twinkling. "I've learnt that it's far easier to keep quiet unless I want a severe scold on the way I spurn good food and starve myself. As you will now see," she added while a small dark woman came bustling out carrying a tray laden with sandwiches, scones, and delectable cakes.

"Now, Miss Frant!" scolded her devoted "daily". "None of your nonsense about dieting and such. I know from the washing up that you hardly eat enough to keep a sparrow alive when I'm not here in the evening! Miss Hilary here – and how are you, miss? – comes from a farm where they know what good teas are. And if I don't see justice done to this one I'll be that offended."

"It looks heaven! But we shall both get fat and die early deaths from heart disease!" Hilary warned.

"Pooh, don't you go talking nonsense to me, Miss Hilary – with Miss Frant here a bag of bones if I don't watch

20

her!" retorted Mrs. Elleray, whose daily help and cooking combined with a fond bullying of her young employer.

She went in, closing the door decisively, and Frant chuckled.

"See how I'm tyrannised!" she remarked. "The dear old thing is as bad as any nannie." She poured out tea, handing Hilary a cup and saucer. "Now of course the doctor's housekeeper really was his nannie, wasn't she?"

"Yes; and seldom lets him forget it," Hilary laughed. "She worked for his mother in Scotland. Sometimes I think she's the only living person who can manage him."

"Is that so? What about his secretary?" Frant raised an eyebrow.

Hilary shook her head, colouring slightly. "I'm only the dogsbody," she replied. "If ever I were so rash as to demand just what time he expected to be in – to sign his letters, for instance – I should expect, and probably receive, a crashing snub."

This time Frant raised both her brows. "You picture a martinet! Yet he can be charming enough when he likes. No 'bedside manner' either."

"Oh, of course. Don't think I'm criticising him, even to you," Hilary told her rather hastily. "As for martinets, I came across some real ones during my training days. Beasts some of them were too," she added reminiscently, and then changing the subject: "I wonder if John will be able to get away and help us eat this splendid tea?"

But half an hour passed without young Mr. Dallam making an appearance: a sure sign, his heartless lady-love observed, of his being involved with customers.

"Never mind, I've been tempted quite enough to satisfy your kind tyrant." Hilary glanced at her wrist-watch. "I must be getting along. Thanks for the hospitality, lovey – I shan't want any supper tonight."

Retracing her steps towards the village a few minutes

later, Hilary took a turning to the right past several grey stone houses which stood back in their gardens. Then, looming just ahead, a pleasant Georgian house in biscuit-coloured stucco stood on a slight rise above a winding drive, a wisteria budding above its graceful, pillared front door with an elegantly designed fanlight. This was universally known as "The Doctor's", and the surgery in a wing added during the last century was familiar to every villager from childhood upwards. There were no surgery hours today, and the doctor's car was absent from the garage. Going up the shallow steps and into the square hallway, Hilary made her way across to the room she used as an office, and going across to her desk, took the cover off the typewriter.

There was a pile of notes to be typed for a pamphlet on which the doctor was engaged, and a sheaf of letters; for in this wide-flung practice, rural though it was, secretarial work was of the first importance. With two child patients in an intensive care unit so far away as Liverpool, and nearer at hand several adult cases in a clinic in Windermere, there were constant reports and other correspondence to deal with. She had been working for over an hour when the sound of a car being driven up to the house came vaguely to her ears. But still deep in her work she went on with steady persistence, only looking up with a start when at the opening of the room door she found a tall figure standing beside her desk.

It was a very tall figure – over six foot two and with shoulders that proclaimed that their owner was still a more than useful rugger forward in a hospital match; the tweeds he nearly always wore held a masculine tang of heather, the clean-scrubbed doctor's hands – strong, well-shaped hands, faintly redolent of the pine disinfectant he had used not long since: both mingled with the expensive pipe tobacco which was one of his only extravagances.

Her slightly startled gaze travelled up to that square-jawed, bronzed face under a shock of crisply curling brown hair streaked with tawny-gold, cut shorter than the usual fashion; intense sherry-coloured eyes stared frowningly down at her, faint lines of fatigue between them and at the corners of a mouth that could be humorous but which just now were set into grimly uncompromising lines.

"Why on earth are you working here this evening – and at this hour?" demanded Blake Kinross. That faint frown of strain and tiredness was deep between his strongly marked brows, but looking up at him she failed to notice those signs of fatigue in her somewhat formidable employer. Before she could answer he added sharply: "Surely there's not so much to do that you couldn't finish at the right time?"

His dry, rather sarcastic tone brought a vivid flush of colour to her cheeks, and it took all her will-power to bite back a hot answer. She said quietly:

"I couldn't. I took the afternoon off, as you must know. But I remembered that you wanted these notes—" Rather defiantly she held up the finished typescript, "and while I was here I thought I might as well finish these few letters as well." Even while she carefully controlled her hand from shaking with annoyance she thought furiously: *"He obviously thinks that if I organised my work properly I needn't be here at all tonight!"*

"Very well." He took the notes from her. "But go home now, for goodness' sake. When I want you to work overtime, I'll tell you. Goodnight." And striding through the communicating door which led to the next room he shut it with a definite click.

Aware of her own temper simmering to boiling point at the unexpectedness of – well, one could only call it his comprehensive snub (which in view of her coming back to get ahead with his work was a bit much!), Hilary's charming mouth set in a tight line, and while she finished the letter in the machine her fingers attacked the unoffending typewriter with unusual venom. She ripped out the letter, separated top paper and carbon with such force that it tore; and then in the act of murmuring a most unfeminine expletive, the memory of how tired and drawn he had looked suddenly damped her own righteous indignation.

Drat the man! But wherever he had been, probably to some patient in an outlying part of the dale, obviously he had been left tired to the point of irritability and exhaustion.

In that case, instead of scolding his hard-working secretary, why the heck couldn't he relax and get himself the drink and supper which Mrs. Tyson would have waiting for him? She put the cover on the machine and pushing her chair back, rose and went across to where she had put down her bag. But before she could pick it up the telephone on her desk began to ring shrilly.

Turning back, she lifted the instrument. "Doctor Kinross's secretary speaking—"

"Oh, is that you, Miss Talgarth? Could I speak to the doctor, please? It's urgent."

"Perhaps I can be of help. If you would tell me what's wrong, Mrs. Wyburn?"

"The most dreadful pains—they came on all of a sudden ten minutes ago. And I'm out of the medicine the doctor gave me—"

Hilary's fingers tightened about the telephone and she suppressed an exasperated sigh. Old Mrs. Wyburn, who lived above the Raise beyond her own home, was not only the village hypochondriac, but perhaps the champion of that tiresome tribe in the whole North-West! She said patiently:

"I'm afraid the doctor is not available just at the moment." (Surely this could wait until that obviously over-tired young man had had something to eat!) "Have you been sick or felt sick at all?" (After all, one must make absolutely sure that the old nuisance wasn't, for once in a way, telling the truth . . .)

"Oh, no, not sick," was the reassuring answer. "Just terribly queer. If I could speak to the doctor—"

"I'll tell him as soon as possible," Hilary answered. Mrs. Wyburn had had fits of being "terribly queer" for somewhere round the last forty years and was still managing to be a hale and hearty seventy-eight. She added conscientiously: "No dizzy spells, I hope?"

"Worse than that – Oh, a terrible queer feeling!" quacked the extremely strong voice through the telephone. "You will tell the doctor, won't you, dear?"

Hilary assured the caller that she would, and as she replaced the instrument the door opened, and Blake Kinross looked in frowningly.

"Did I hear the telephone?" he demanded.

"Yes; it was old Mrs. Wyburn complaining of one of her usual 'queer turns', I made sure it was the usual, and said I would tell you when you were available. There's not the slightest need to put off your much-needed dinner," Hilary told him. "Another bottle of bismuth mixture tomorrow will keep her quite happy."

Instead of agreeing he stared at her, his dark brows drawn together.

"And supposing that for once there was something wrong? Since when have you taken it on yourself to decide for me?"

She flushed, meeting his cold glance, her own steady. "There's nothing wrong with her, and you know it."

"I shall know better when I've found out." He turned back to the inner room, and she heard him fastening the leather bag that always accompanied him on visits to patients.

Drawing a deep breath, she decided to ignore the manifestly unfair reaction to her attempt at protecting him from his most exasperating patient. But before he could pick up his case a new ally appeared in the small but formidable shape of ex-Nannie, now Mrs. Tyson, the housekeeper.

"And where are you off to just as dinner is ready, may I ask, Mr. Blake?" she demanded, erupting from the direction of the kitchen quarters. "A nice fillet of sole and steak and kidney pie to follow – if you let the sole spoil for anything less than a life-and-death call I'll never forgive you!"

"You will, you know." The doctor's stern face softened into an amused smile as he met the faded blue, accusing stare of his ex-nannie. "I won't be long. Just a quick check-up on old Mrs. Wyburn – yes, I know," he added as Mrs. Tyson opened her mouth in imminent wrath: "But I've got to make sure."

"Oh, well! If you *will* encourage her—" Mrs. Tyson bustled away to do what she could to keep the meal from spoiling, and Blake Kinross glanced across at his secretary, an eyebrow slightly raised, his former annoyance giving place to a somewhat rueful smile.

"Of course she doesn't believe there's a thing wrong, any more than you do," he said. "I'm sorry if I was a bit short, but we can't be too sure, you know."

Hilary refused to respond to that unbending, and turned to take up her bag and gloves. "I'm sorry I – interfered."

"Your turn to snub me," he said with that lightning change of mood she had so often found disconcerting. Looking up now, she had to respond to an undoubtedly very charming smile, even while she said coldly:

"You're quite right, of course. There might be something really amiss, but I'm so used to her I discounted any possibility. Which probably shows I should have made a bad nurse."

"With experience I'm sure you would have made an

excellent nurse," he said coolly. "Come along, I'll be passing your home. You must be wanting your own meal."

To have said she preferred to walk would have been ungracious as well as untruthful. She accepted his offer with cool politeness and then, being a naturally sweet-tempered person, gave an inward laugh and a mental shake, setting herself to respond affably to the doctor's peace overtures while he drove his car through the village and over the bridge on which she and Frant had paused earlier. Another five minutes and they were before the gate that led to the patch of flower garden in front of Willowbeck Farm.

He braked the car to a halt, and as she opened the door beside her, she said calmly:

"Thank you for the lift home. I hope you'll find all is well with Mrs. Wyburn."

"And if I don't you'll be more than surprised," he suggested, smiling at her.

"Certainly I shall," she agreed. "I know it's not my place to say it, but I do urge you not to let her keep you so long that your dinner will be quite spoiled!"

"Don't rub it in!" He raised a hand in farewell as he started the car again. "If that's the case you may comfort yourself with the scold I shall get from Nannie Tyson! Goodnight."

He was gone almost before she could reply, and looking after the vanishing rear-light as it vanished up the twilit Fell road, a half reluctant smile touched Hilary's lips. Really! Sometimes she wondered why she continued to put up with those sudden moods. But though he was often difficult, sometimes impossible, he could also be – disarming. Anyway, bother him.

Dinner was not quite ready when she entered the lamp-lit, oak-panelled room with its diamond-paned windows across which curtains of flowered chintz were drawn. Fine linen mats and gleaming silver and glass glowed a welcome on the four-hundred-year-old gate-legged table polished by generations of loving hands to a golden satin finish. Though they took most of their meals farming style on a spotless cloth, in the evening Hilary liked to keep up a more formal ritual, as had her mother before her – not out of any snobbishness, but from a knowledge that it pleased Cousin Priscilla, and gave her and her brother a relaxation from the often arduous labours of the day in these few hours they spent together.

Tim Talgarth, her senior by three years, a broad-shouldered young man with a lean, handsome face, looked round in the act of pouring out sherry at an oaken side table, and grinned across at her.

"Just in time for a glass of what cheers Auntie!" he observed. "I wondered if you'd have a meal at either Frant's or the doctor's. But," he added rather mischievously as Cousin Priscilla bustled in with a loaded tray bearing a magnificent steak and kidney pie accompanied by vegetables from the garden, "I see that you dared not offer such treachery to the Willowbeck kitchens!"

"Beast!" his sister observed without heat as she accepted a glass of sherry and Mrs. Brathay bustled about the table. "He's trying to make out I don't like your cooking best, Cousin Priscilla! Mr. Hardisty was saying it doesn't seem such a long twenty years since he was about to celebrate his fifth birthday! And if you ask me, he's every bit as detestable as he was then."

"Yes? But at least I no longer put tadpoles in my dear sister's bed," Tim pointed out.

"No, but you're not so much older for all that," Cousin Priscilla retorted, beaming indulgently. "Now come along, both of you, and eat up your nice dinner before it gets cold!"

"Snubbed again!" Tim took his place at the head of the table. But his sister was suddenly aware of a somewhat

28

penetrating gaze bent on her. "So you really like your job with Blake Kinross, Hilary?"

"Of course I do." She sipped her sherry a little defiantly. "Why shouldn't I?"

"Only that I've sometimes wondered." Tim sipped his own wine reflectively. "After all, he *is* a brilliant sort of bloke – far more than we deserve up here. It's a wonder he doesn't shake the dust of Tarnmere from his well polished boots and take up his quarters in London's Harley Street – which is where, I gather, he really ought to have been."

Hilary thought her brother's sudden observations no longer had the power to startle her, but suddenly found she was mistaken. "What makes you say that?" she demanded.

Tim shrugged his big shoulders. "I met a fellow in Carlisle the other day – rather an important medico, studying some bug the miners are prone to round the Cumberland coast. When he found out I was from Tarnmere, he was full of praise for Kinross, wondering why he wanted to bury himself in our fells and 'waste his talent' as he put it, quite without meaning offence! I told him that was the chap's own affair, and our gain." Serving steak and kidney with a lavish hand, he changed the subject. "Did you know Hollins Hall has been let at last? To some enormously rich personage who's bringing his wife to live amongst us, anyway for part of the year. So that will be something new for the village gossips to get their teeth into."

"Really? Who are they?" Hilary asked with more interest than she really felt.

"No idea," her brother returned. "But no doubt we shall soon see. I believe they're expected some time this week."

Going up to bed later, Hilary was aware that it was her brother's casual remarks about Blake Kinross which filled her mind – though why they should do so, she told herself

29

in a spurt of unexpected irritation, she didn't know. Any more than she knew why her employer should have filled her thoughts so often and so much lately – unless it was the irritation he quite often caused her.

With which slightly indignant thought she fell asleep: only to have a dark, attractive face with a strong jaw, and that undoubtedly musical voice, haunt her dreams with a persistence that brought more than passing annoyance to her waking consciousness.

The next morning she was busy sorting the post when Blake Kinross came into her office.

She returned his "Good morning" with cool courtesy.

"Lady Blakeney telephoned ten minutes ago," she informed him. "She is sorry to be tiresome, but her lumbago is – in her own words – 'playing old Harry' with her, and do you think you could look in later in the day, after surgery hours?"

"I'll call in about tea-time so long as no emergency crops up," he answered, taking the sheaf of letters she brought across to him. Seating himself at his desk, he looked up with a sudden cock of his left eyebrow accompanying the glint of a somewhat rueful smile: "A trifle ironic, I think you'll agree – but the lady of the Manor is far less imperative in her summons than old Mrs. Wyburn in her cottage over the Raise." And while Hilary glanced up with a non-committal smile: "You were quite right, of course – there wasn't a thing wrong with the old . . . lady."

"Yes, but I still wasn't right to interfere," Hilary returned. "She'll cry 'wolf' once too often at her age. You had to make sure."

"So I did. But it's rather noble of you to admit it," he agreed.

His tone was friendly enough, but Hilary, suddenly aware of being far more sensitive than she had any need to be, thought she could detect a faint note of sarcasm and felt the colour rising in her cheeks. Luckily he was not looking at her, but going through the letters she had handed him. She had time to give herself an angry mental shake. What on earth was up with her? It couldn't have mattered less – and yet here she was, inflating a trivial subject which should have been lightly dismissed in that casual exchange.

She said: "There's an invitation to attend that conference in London you mentioned the other day. Sir Henry Hargreaves seems very anxious that you should go."

He looked up quickly. "Does he, indeed? That's something of a compliment from the Great Man who was my boss – to remember a North-County G.P. I shall have to go of course. Take a letter now, will you – ?"

Opening her shorthand notebook, Hilary was suddenly remembering a passage from a letter she had received only the other day. It had been from a friend, a fellow nurse at her own hospital, who had written:

"So you are working for Blake Kinross! He was something of a pet protegé of our big man here at St. Blaise's – Sir Henry Hargreaves whom everyone adores and calls 'Sir Harry' behind his handsome back. My dear! Six foot three, with a mane of grey hair and the most devastatingly handsome profile, never mind the fact that he's rising sixty! He's been heard to regret the fact that 'young Kinross' decided, on his uncle's death, to take up the reins on your native heath. But apparently his family have been doctors in Cumberland and Westmorland for a hundred and fifty years or thereabouts, so I suppose it's a case of family tradition winning over Harley Street where Blake Kinross was fully expected to land. It seems your dalesfolk have had a stroke of more than ordinary medical luck."

As her employer's attractive voice began to dictate, she resolutely banished everything but the task in hand from

31

her mind. An hour later he had to drive over to Windermere to see a patient, and for Hilary the rest of the morning passed in typing, answering telephone calls and making notes on matters to be attended to on Blake's return after lunch.

Surgery hours began at three o'clock when the waiting-room would be fairly well filled – not to overflowing, thank goodness, that would come later when days occurred of treacherously brief warmth in which people would leave off winter-weight clothes, and season colds and rheumatism would revenge themselves on the rash ones.

But the expected routine of a Tuesday afternoon was destined to be rudely interrupted. Blake returned from Windermere by half past two, having lunched early with a fellow doctor. He was making out several prescriptions which had to be posted to or called for by cases not in need of immediate personal attention, when the telephone on his desk rang shrilly.

Laying down his pen, he picked up the instrument.

"Dr. Kinross speaking—"

He listened for a few moments, and Hilary busy at her own desk paid no attention, until a sharp exclamation made her look up quickly.

"What! Would you mind repeating that? Yes. On Dunster Raise . . . near the foot of Cowbiggin Hill . . . Down the thirty-foot embankment. How many casualties? . . . Difficult to tell . . . I see . . . probably between twenty-five and thirty, possibly more . . . Many children? Very well, I'll notify Keswick and Kendal Hospitals as well as Windermere, we shall want all the beds we can get, and none of them have many available . . . Of course, I'll come along at once. Would you contact any farmers or other people you know to have cars? Thank you, Mrs. Dalston, you've done splendidly – just carry on with the good work, please—"

32

He replaced the telephone, his face set and grim.

Hilary was already on her feet. "What's happened?"

"An accident on Dunster Raise. The Keswick bus skidded near the foot of Cowbiggin Hill going down from the Raise, and plunged down the embankment into one of Mr. Gregson's fields," he answered curtly. "Apparently it somersaulted and then landed up against that thick belt of hazel trees. Thank God there's no wall just there." He was dialling a number while he spoke. "Get me the necessary bandages and dressings – antiseptics, syringes and morphia – I shan't have enough in my usual case, so ransack the surgery . . . St. Anne's Cottage Hospital? Dr. Kinross speaking—"

While he gave brief, clear instructions, Hilary hurried through to the surgery, sorting out the necessary medical equipment with deft, steady hands, her training asserting itself in the sudden ice-cold clarity that every nurse must learn in the first weeks of hospital life, or fail from the start.

In a very few minutes Blake had finished his three telephone calls, pulled on a heavy mackintosh – for the morning's rain had returned in force and was pelting down out of a misty grey sky that hid the mountain peaks – and was taking his own shabby case out to the car when she joined him.

"The surgery patients will have to be told to come back tomorrow," he said.

"Mrs. Tyson can attend to that," Hilary told him. "I'm coming with you."

He hesitated, turning in the open doorway. "I'd certainly be glad of your help, but—"

"Of course I'm coming." She was struggling into her raincoat. "You know Nurse Rossiter is out at Ellerbeck Farm with Mrs. Bryant this afternoon." Nurse Rossiter was the district nurse. "They've no telephone there, and it will take ages to contact her. Oh, Mrs. Tyson, a quick word with you."

Leaving her to apprise the housekeeper of what had happened and give some instructions, Blake went out to the car, turning up his collar against the Lakeland downpour. His shoes had been exchanged just inside the front door for a pair of hefty gumboots, and squelching out to the streaming car he would have looked more like a farmer than a doctor to southern eyes, but as with everyone else in these parts the rains were so much a part of life as to occasion neither comment nor annoyance.

Hilary was silent while her employer negotiated the rather tricky turning out from the short drive into the rain-washed road beyond. Then she said rather hesitantly:

"Did Mrs. Dalston say whether there were many people – badly injured?"

"She didn't think so, but naturally couldn't be sure – she's already had three who were able to walk safe in her cottage at the foot of the hill," Blake answered. "Thank heaven the engine didn't catch fire." A worried frown creased his brows. "I wish we could get some more help – the hospitals will be sending ambulances as soon as they can, but this weather doesn't make swift driving easy."

"No, and the nearest of them is ten miles away. I wonder who we could rope in—" She broke off. They were passing the road which led past John Dallam's antique shop, the interior of which was lit against the greyness of the afternoon. She saw his estate car parked before the open front doorway, and framed against the glow was John himself, and the slight, smaller figure of Frant talking to him.

"Why, there's Frant!" Hilary exclaimed. "Do stop a minute, please. I know she's learnt first-aid and she's absolutely level-headed in an emergency. And John's car would be more than useful."

"Excellent idea." Blake slowed his car to a crawl. "Give them a hail, will you?"

34

At the sound of Hilary's voice calling the two in the doorway turned. Frant waved, then seeing her friend beckon hurried out, putting up an umbrella.

"Hullo there. Anything wrong?" she asked. Then as Hilary explained hurriedly, John Dallam, who had followed his beloved, loomed enormous in oilskins, rubber boots and sou'wester, exclaiming:

"A bus overturned on the Raise? That's bad. We'll be right along – I'm not up to Frant's standard in first-aid, but I can do my bit."

"Fine!" Blake approved, and set his car in motion again, but not before he heard Frant say:

"Lucky you got those new tyres the other day – we don't want to skid and add to the casualties."

Once clear of the village Blake was able to get up speed on the broad, straight road which ran upwards towards the eminence known as Dunster's Raise leading northwards away from Tarnmere. Gaining the ridge was a blustery business with squalls of rain buffeting the car, and the mountains on either side invisible save for their lower slopes across which wreaths of coiling mist wound like phantom snakes over the greystone walls, many of which sheltered groups of hardy Herdwick sheep.

The other side of the Raise, known as Cowbiggin Hill, seemed to be alive with vehicles, proclaiming that the dalesmen who had already heard of the accident were rallying valiantly to the rescue. Among the dozen or so cars parked at the foot of the hill Hilary at once recognised her brother's, and Tim was one of the party alongside the long green single-decker bus which had plunged into a hazel coppice across a field scored by tyre marks and the churning up of mud where the big vehicle had performed a complete somersault, landing with its front wheels deep in mire, its rear bucking at an alarming angle skywards.

Scrambling down the embankment would have been a

tricky business at any time, but now it was rendered doubly so by the mud and teeming rain. Some of the passengers had been extricated and escorted to the parked cars, where many at least were in shelter, though badly shocked and in need of attention. But along the edge of the field where the bus had landed were several people, obvious stretcher-cases, sheltered by umbrellas held by kindly farmers and their womenfolk. There was the sound of a child crying, and a woman's half-hysterical moaning from within the bus.

Seeing the tall form of the doctor approaching, the men gathered about the wrecked vehicle parted, and while Hilary stumbled after him, she heard her brother explain:

"We didn't dare to get them all out – I've been in myself, and I'm afraid there are at least four with broken legs, and others who may be worse hurt. The poor fellow we're really worried about is the driver – he's unconscious and jammed in the cabin."

"I've telephoned the fire brigade, and Dalston's garage are on their way with help, but until we get some cutting gear here we can do nothing much." The uniformed figure of Sergeant Renfrew, the local policeman, loomed out of the murk. Then seeing Blake he went on in a lowered voice: "Thank God you've come, Doctor. The poor chap's in a pretty bad way, I reckon. And he's showing signs of recovering consciousness – which may be good in one way, but he's in bad pain—"

Blake was already half way through the shattered window of the buckled door. There was a faint moan, and then in a few moments he dropped back on to the muddy churned-up grass, his face grim.

"So far as I can make out under these conditions he's more than lucky to be alive," he said tersely, opening his case. "An umbrella, one of you, please – will you hold this torch, Miss Talgarth?"

It was anything but easy preparing the syringe, let

alone administering the morphia to the injured man, but Blake managed it with extraordinary deftness, speaking a few comforting words as the unfortunate driver half came to his senses. Then, just before hoisting himself with the help of several burly and mackintoshed figures into the back of the bus, he turned to Hilary again.

"I see Miss Frant and young Dallam coming down," he said. "Will you ask them to attend to as many of the shock cases in the cars as possible, then perhaps you would join me in here."

"O.K., Doctor." The intervening months seemed to have slipped away into nothingness, and but for the absence of a uniform it was once again Nurse Talgarth who spoke. She plunged along to where Frant and John Dallam were coming down the embankment, and when she told them what was needed, they turned and scrabbled painfully up the bank again.

"Here, wait a minute!" Hilary called. "You'd better take what you'll need from my case here."

"Oh, drat – go back and get what's wanted, John," Frant commanded, breathlessly.

John paused, his boots planted as firmly as he could manage in the mud. "I've got some things in my old bus, but I suppose they won't be sufficient—"

"Here you are." Hilary lurched forwards, carrying a case. "I've got plenty more stuff down here, so you can take this lot. But for heaven's sake don't drop it."

"That'll be O.K. – so long as I don't take a tumble," John replied, and taking out the packets of dressing and bottles she handed him, stowed them away in the enormous flapped pockets on each side of his oilskin.

"Coom on, lad!" rumbled an elderly farmer whose burly figure was even bigger than John's. "I'll gie thee a hand oop. Likely tha' doesn' have the trick o' climbing mucky slopes like this. Gie us your fist, lad—"

Hilary turned back to the wrecked bus. By this time

Blake had disappeared inside, and it was her turn to be hoisted up, clasping more of the precious surgical and medical equipment securely against herself.

It was Tim himself who came forward and heaved her up in his arms with an understanding brotherly grin. "Mind how you go, Sis," he warned. "There are only about eight left inside, but some are in a pretty poor way. This big torch be of any help?"

"Thanks – just what I want." Hilary took it gratefully and, as Blake administered pain-killing injections and soothing words, braced herself to help all she could, realising with pity that three of the remaining victims were elderly and as much frightened as in pain.

It seemed a century before ambulance men arrived with stretchers and trained skill to get the worst cases to hospital. There had been nearly forty people in the crowded bus, and it was little short of a miracle that not only were the majority of the injured walking cases, but there had not been one fatality.

By the time equipment had arrived to free the driver, it was dark and the rain still pelting down. The brilliant headlights of several cars were trained on the scene from the foot of the hill, and at last the injured man was safely on a stretcher. He was only semi-conscious, but he asked faintly: "What about the others? Are they – is it very bad?"

Blake bent over him, his deep voice gentle and reassuring.

"No fatal casualties – and as for yourself, we'll have you fit as ever in a few weeks, you're not going to blot your copybook by doing anything but getting better quickly—"

The driver slipped into unconsciousness again with a faint sigh that told of infinite relief. Hilary, who had been priding herself on the steadiness of her nerves, felt a sudden different sense of triumph. How wonderful it was to see what comfort and assurance Blake Kinross was capable of bringing to those in pain and fear. No doubt about his vocation! A born, dedicated doctor—

The thought broke at the sound of her name, and turning she found her brother beside her.

"You must be worn out," Tim said. "Will the doc let me run you home now, or will you be wanted some more?"

"Of course I shall," she replied quickly. "I'll be back later. Don't worry about me. I'm – fine."

"All right, if you say so." Then as Blake called to her Tim disappeared into the darkness.

"Was that your brother?" he asked, glancing into the shadows. "Would you rather go home with him? I must get along to the hospital in case I'm wanted."

"Can I come too?" she asked. "They're short-staffed, you know—"

It was too dark to see his expression, and he sounded almost curt as he agreed: "Good. Come along, then. That is, if you're really not too tired."

"Not a bit," she lied stoutly, and followed him up the dark, slippery bank. On the road again Blake paused to exchange a word with a group of half a dozen of the helpers left, when with startling suddenness a big car loomed out of the darkness, its powerful headlights illumining the entire scene.

As the uniformed chauffeur brought the Rolls to a halt, Hilary saw into the luxury of the lighted interior from which a man's burly figure spoke through a lowered window:

"Anything wrong here? Has there been an accident? Can we do anything to help?" The speaker's tone was rather harsh with a note of impatience, as though help was offered with reluctance.

A farmer who stood nearest the newcomers answered: "All O.K. now, sir, thank you all the same. A bus plunged down the embankment, but the injured are safely away, and we're just going home ourselves."

Before the man in the car could reply, a woman's clear, rather brittle voice exclaimed:

"Good heavens! What an awful thing to happen! Are you really sure there's nothing we can do?"

"They've just said so, my dear," the first speaker told her. "Drive on, Charles—"

"Wait!" his companion commanded imperiously, thrusting him away. "Is there anyone we could give a lift to? We're going to Tarnmere—"

It was then that Hilary became aware of Blake standing very still beside her, his eyes fixed on the girl whose face had now taken the place of her companion's at the lowered window. The lamps of the Rolls were flooding the long stretch of road rising ahead, and everyone could be seen clearly. But it seemed to Hilary that Blake was only aware of the lovely face looking out at them. He stepped back, almost as though he had been shot, and his own face, which had been drawn and tired, was suddenly white as paper, his eyes staring incredulously into the Rolls.

"Thank you, ma'am, but we've got all our cars. No need to trouble yourself," the farmer returned, glancing towards the doctor, perhaps a little surprised at his silence.

Then as the girl in the car continued to lean forward, Hilary saw her clearly for the first time. She was quite startlingly beautiful, her gold hair shining above the perfect oval of her face, a half-smile on lips that were both passionate and wilful, her eyes glittering a strange greenish colour in the glow of the car's lighted interior. Then with a brief "Goodnight," she sank back into her seat, the Rolls moved silently up the hill, and it was as though a picture flung suddenly on a screen had faded out.

There was a moment's silence, then one of the men gave a whistle, exclaiming:

"Some good-looker! Who'd she be?"

There was a laugh and an appreciative murmur, but

40

looking again at Blake, Hilary was oddly disturbed to see that he still stood like a man turned to stone, that strange, almost stricken expression on his face.

Then, as if suddenly wakening to consciousness of his surroundings, he straightened abruptly and striding to his car, got in.

Following, Hilary was almost sure he had forgotten all about her; and while they travelled swiftly through the night she was asking herself with a strange feeling of apprehension why the glimpse of that unknown girl should have affected him so strangely. The girl had not even noticed him, but did he know her? And why had the sight of her affected him as strongly as it had undoubtedly done?

Anyhow, Hilary told herself, there was no reason why his evident emotion should disturb her. And yet she knew she was disturbed, with a depth of uneasiness that there was no accounting for.

For it could not be denied that, whatever meaning might lie behind it, that fleeting glimpse of the lovely passenger in the Rolls-Royce had given Dr. Kinross a shock which had gone near to being – overwhelming.

CHAPTER THREE

HOURS – it seemed more like whole centuries later – with long and arduous hospital work behind them, the drive back to Tarnmere was accomplished in almost complete silence. Both were too tired to exchange anything but the briefest of comments; but stealing a look at the strong profile of the man beside her, his long-fingered doctor's hands gripping the wheel, Hilary found that she could not control an odd tug of anxiety at her heart. The crease between his strongly marked brows was naturally accounted for by weariness – for heaven knew he had been, like herself, working all out for longer than it seemed possible to imagine. And yet his half frown accompanied by a grimness in the set of his jaw, a tension she had not sensed in him before, was, she felt certain, caused by that brief encounter on Cowbiggin Hill.

He seemed sunk in a reverie, to have gone a thousand miles away; until with a sudden turn of his head and a half smile at her, he forced himself out of whatever thoughts had taken so strongly hold of him.

"You must be terribly tired," he said, unconsciously echoing her brother's accusation in what now seemed another existence. "But I'm afraid there are still a few ends to be tied up. Do you feel you can cope?"

"Of course!" She smiled at him, and suddenly he was thinking how very relaxed she was as well as capable. He was perfectly aware that she too had been stretched to the utmost during these last hours of unremitting strain, and yet she showed no sign of it. What a darned shame she had not been able to go forward with her chosen career of nursing – for if ever anyone had proved themselves everything a doctor could desire in a grim emergency, Hilary Talgarth had done so tonight.

The thought was involuntary, for Blake Kinross was not one of those doctors who were apt to look on nursing staff as so many automata; he was ready to give honour where honour was due: a fact which had endeared him to many feminine hearts that beat beneath starched aprons!

Now he had broken that long silence she felt that it would be as well to make an attempt at easing the tension in which he seemed to have encased himself. She said:

"How splendid everyone was. Things might have been so much worse without all those willing helpers. Though," she added with quiet pride, "it's no more than one would have expected of Tarnmere folk."

He turned his head and in the dim light from the dashboard she saw that he was smiling. "Indeed it isn't. And what sterling work young Dallam and your artist friend did. That young woman is a tower of strength."

"She is indeed. I had a word with her, and she said she was taking John back to have supper – a reward that couldn't be bettered," Hilary laughed. "Which reminds me – it isn't quite suppertime yet – or is it?"

"Let's see!" He leaned forward, switching on a stronger light. "I rather think – as the moralists are fond of saying – it's later than you think!"

"Good heavens!" She stared at the clock before her. "Past half-past nine already – it can't be true!"

"Indeed it is. You're forgetting it took the best part of an hour to cut that poor driver fellow free of his cabin," Blake answered. "And before that we had all those other cases. Getting them safely away to hospital took double time in this filthy weather, and we've been doing hospital work ourselves for some time, with only sandwiches and strong tea from Matron to sustain us! You'd better telephone your brother when we get back, and tell him you'll be having some food with me. Then I'll run you home when the rest of our work is done – which won't be until very late indeed, I'm afraid—"

He proved a true prophet, and their final arrival at his house was as welcome to Hilary as a harbour to travellers after storm and tempest.

Until they gained the warmth and dryness of soft golden lamplight, and a welcoming fire lit by Mrs. Tyson against the chill of the teeming and pitch black night, it seemed that cold and wet was something which had gone on for so long that it must last indefinitely. It was sheer heaven to shed one's soaking raincoat and muddy boots; to dry hair that was streaming under the quite inadequate headscarf she had hastily donned such a long time before. And for once to accept a steaming hot whisky and lemon (a drink she normally detested) and feel blessed heat coursing through her chilled veins seemed something very near to heaven.

Suddenly the northern wind which still whined tempestuously down from the darkened mountains, bending the tender-leafed trees and sending cold cloud-wrack across the chill quarter moon that peered intermittently through darkness, was something that no longer mattered. Triumph became involved in the day's disaster which might have been so much worse, in the knowledge that all concerned were warm and dry, and safe – including themselves.

But even safe arrival had given a great deal of work to Dr. Kinross and his assistant. A series of telephone calls to the various hospitals which had taken in the casualties; calls to other doctors; anxious relatives to be reassured and comforted; the local Press to be dealt with and courteously persuaded that it would be far better to refrain from sending eager reporters to garner information that night: that it would be infinitely to their advantage, both from a humanistic and journalistic point of view, to garner their much-needed information the following day.

It was quarter to eleven before all was done and there was any chance of relaxation; by that time both Blake and

44

Hilary were conscious of utter exhaustion which made the mere thought of food distasteful. But Mrs. Tyson bustled in and announced firmly that a late supper would be ready in twenty minutes, and when they tried to protest, both were firmly put in their place.

"Now that's quite enough nonsense!" she said severely. "After all you've gone through, the idea of not keeping up your strength! You will do as you're told, both of you, or I shall be very angry indeed!"

And not deigning to wait for a reply she went out, shutting the door firmly behind her.

Blake sighed, and then laughed wearily. "The nannie has got the upper hand of the housekeeper tonight!" he observed. "But do you know, I rather agree with her."

"But I ought to get straight home," Hilary protested. "Now that everything is settled—"

"Nonsense! Finish that whisky, and wait to see what Nannie Tyson has for us," he ordered. "And I do beg of you not to argue. I'm much too tired."

She laughed, but sensing the fatigue behind his words, obeyed. And by the time the housekeeper had laid a table for two in front of the fire, she found her appetite had magically returned with the serving of steaming bowls of soup, fragrant with meat and vegetables and barley, that made an ideal prelude to delicious omelettes filled and garnished with asparagus tips, followed by a very light sweet, a delicately flavoured orange water-ice.

During the meal conversation was desultory, but somehow neither felt the need of making social observations. They only knew that firelight and good food, suitable to tiredness and the lateness of hour, made the mud and wet and cold of the unpleasant day they had been through seem to belong to another world.

"Ah! That's better!" Mrs. Tyson observed with a beam of satisfaction. "Brought the roses back into your cheeks.

And now here's some of that coffee which can't keep you awake, however much you have of it!"

"You spoil us, Tysie," Blake told her, using a nursery name that made the old housekeeper bridle with pleasure. "That was a meal out of this world!"

"Indeed it was!" Hilary confirmed warmly. "I've never been so spoiled in years! Cousin Priscilla will be green with envy when she hears of this evening!"

"Go along with you, Miss Hilary! You just drink your coffee while it's nice and hot, and then Mr. Blake – I should say, the doctor – will drive you safely home."

"So I will!" Blake agreed, and as the door shut behind the old lady: "I think we might now venture a liqueur. Unless you're afraid of ending this evening in a damp ditch!"

Hilary joined in his laughter as he poured out a Drambuie, and at the pretty sound he found himself thinking, quite unexpectedly: *"I've never before known just how restful a girl can be – and how her thoughts can chime in with one's own!"*

But then, through Hilary's mood of quiet contentment, a sudden unwelcome picture rose: the memory of a blonde girl in the softly lit, luxurious interior of a Rolls, leaning forward, a half smile on her lips, the lovely oval of her face framed by the softness of the mink collar that half concealed the magnificent necklet of pearls about the slender column of her throat.

But though she wondered, she did not know how distinctly Blake was also remembering.

Once that picture had meant everything to him – had the power to send his heart pounding wildly in his breast, causing the blood to run like fire through his veins . . .

And then: the bitterness, disillusion, and what he had believed to be heartbreak.

As he gazed into the leaping flames that curled round the logs on the hearth, his mouth and eyes hardened, and unconsciously his fingers tightened about the handle of the cup he was holding.

Watching him from the depth of her chair opposite Hilary saw that hardening, and with sudden swift intuition felt certain he was remembering those moments when he had stood as if turned to stone in the darkness of the road, looking with such intentness at that girl to whom he had remained unseen. His expression, that sudden unnatural stillness which had been so clear to her while she stood beside him in the reflected glow of the car's powerful headlights, remained vividly with her. She had been so strangely troubled by that glimpse of some disturbed depths beyond her knowledge.

Try as she would, she could not keep at bay the questions which came knocking at her mind.

Where had he met that girl before? What was the cause of the shock and – yes, bitterness which had sprung to life in him at the sight of that elegantly lovely vision in the Rolls?

The sound of falling ash from the logs sent a leaping flame into the roon, and putting down her empty coffee cup she said, with a lightness she was far from feeling:

"You know, I really think I ought to be getting home. I can never thank you enough for a lovely supper."

"Time enough for another cup of coffee, then I'll drive you home." He smiled across at her. "It's you I have to thank – for had I been by myself I doubt if I should have eaten a thing. I'm afraid I've been a very dull host—"

"Indeed you haven't. It's sometimes nicer – at least I think so – just to sit and enjoy oneself and not talk much, especially after a tiring day like this one has been," she told him. "But you must certainly not come out again. I can easily walk home."

"Maybe, but you're not going to," he returned with a touch of that cool arrogance which had once had the power to annoy her. Now she only smiled acquiescence.

He rose from his chair a little abruptly, crossing to the long windows and pulling the heavy curtains aside, revealed a night of wind and rain.

"I hope your coat will have dried out by now – the spring seems to have lost itself, and the wind is north-east. Take some extra rest in the morning – you've more than earned it. And I shan't be here until after lunch." Then in response to her enquiring look: "I've got various of the patients to see, particularly the bus driver who, because I got him out, seems to think my appearance necessary as he keeps on asking will I go and see him tomorrow! There are plenty of capable people round him, but I've promised to go; so I shan't be needing you here until the afternoon."

"Very well. But honestly, I don't need extra rest. I'm tougher than you think," she assured him, following him out into the hall.

As they got into the car outside, the wind was howling down from the darkened mountains like the wail of a thousand demons, and jagged cloud-wrack raced across the face of a half moon riding high amidst the tempest-torn sky. But the rain had mercifully ceased, and the drive through the sleeping village up towards Willowbeck Farm was accomplished under a clearing sky that showed the mountain peaks shadowy and far-off, like the landscape of some faintly silvered dream.

Both were very tired, and hardly a word was exchanged before Blake braked the car to a standstill in front of the iron gate leading to Willowbeck Farm's front garden. The long, low white house was quiet under the fitful moonlight, only the glimmer of one window showing Hilary that her brother had been waiting for her return.

Preparing to get out, she turned to her companion. "Thank you so much again for the lovely supper—" she began.

"Thank you – a thousand times," he interrupted.

"You've been – more than a tower of strength. Don't look so surprised!" he laughed. "I may seem to take things for granted, but I'm not ungrateful for very valuable services rendered. Thank you, Hilary." He stretched out his hand, and putting her own into it she realised that it was the first time that he had ever used her Christian name; and to her secret annoyance was conscious of sudden breathlessness as she knew her colour had deepened while the firm pressure of those long, capable fingers still held hers.

"Why, that's quite absurd." She had to stop herself from stammering like a schoolgirl. "Thank goodness I was trained, and could be of some use—" He released his clasp and she opened the door beside her rather hurriedly. "You must be worn out. I hope you'll get a good night's rest."

"Don't worry – I shall," he returned. "Goodnight, and again thank you, Nurse."

"If only I were really just 'Nurse'!" The words were out before she could stop them or repress the bitter note of sadness in her tone.

For a moment he looked at her, then with a jerk the car moved off.

Hilary had not looked back as her employer drove off. Gaining the shelter of the little porch, she entered the stone-flagged hall where a small lamp burnt in readiness for her return; then having locked and bolted the door she took up the lamp and went upstairs.

She paused outside the line of light beneath the door of her brother's room and tapped softly. Receiving no reply, she lifted the latch, peering round, and then laughed under her breath.

Young Farmer Talgarth had fallen asleep over the book which lay on the blue coverlet of his bed. With a lock of hair the same red-gold colour of his sister's falling over his forehead, he looked very much as when he had been the schoolboy of not so long ago; only the lamplight catching the glint of hair on his bronzed chest between his open pyjama jacket, and a touch of blue on his square jaw marked the difference of the years. Hilary laughed again, more audibly, and picking up his book, was turning down the lamp when he stirred and opened his eyes.

"Don't say you've actually come home!" he observed drowsily. "I was getting worried about you, but then I realised you must be carousing with the doctor – at least I hope he gave you something to eat and drink!"

"Both," she assured him, her cheeks taking on a slightly deeper pink, and her brother, observing her from under his long lashes, gave a sleepy but mischievous chuckle.

"One of these fine days," he said on a yawn, "I'm going to lose you to another bloke and be left a lone, lorn bachelor with only Cousin Priscilla to look after me. Pity you're not a bit plainer!"

"Thank you *so* much!" Hilary retorted. "Heaven help the girl mad enough to marry a selfish brute like yourself. Though unfortunately for myself I'm not likely to leave you – as you deserve – just yet."

"In that case," Tim murmured, "make yourself useful by turning out the light . . . Did you have a nice supper with Blake Kinross?"

"Very nice, thank you." Hilary bent over and kissed him sedately on the cheek. "Now go to sleep again."

"Decent sort of chap, that." Tim obediently closed his eyes, only to open them a moment later and gave her an unexpectedly wide-awake and slightly malicious grin. "I like him. And I've a strong idea you do too, dear Sis!"

Without deigning to reply but with a considerably heightened colour, she turned out the lamp on his bedside table and going to the door, closed it with a decided snap. A sleepy laugh pursued her to her own room, but that too was something it was quite easy – at this time of night – haughtily to ignore!

CHAPTER FOUR

ALTHOUGH she had no intention of doing so, Hilary slept late into the next morning. It had been perhaps over-tiredness which had caused her to remain wakeful for some time after her head rested on the pillow; and when finally sleep came it was broken by uneasy dreams in which she was following Blake in a car but never able to catch up with him, even though it was urgent in some vague but disturbing way to warn him against a girl with corn-gold hair who was bringing disaster into his life.

But at last deep exhaustion had overwhelmed uneasy dreams; and the next thing she knew was that the door opened to reveal Cousin Priscilla on the threshold bearing a laden breakfast tray. A second and horrified stare at the clock beside her showed that the hands pointed to quarter to ten.

"Good heavens!" Hilary sat bolt upright, dashing the sleep from her eyes, her glance at Mrs. Brathay reproachful. "How *could* you let me oversleep like this?"

"The doctor rang, and told me to remind you that he won't be there until this afternoon, and you're on no account to go along until after lunch! I looked in earlier, but Tim said not to disturb you, and for once I agreed with both men – which makes history! So just relax and let me shake up your pillows, and then you'll eat these nice scrambled eggs with chopped bacon – there's porridge if you want it, but porridge in bed I can't abide myself! But there's fresh orange juice and the best marmalade with freshly baked baps."

Hilary leant back, regarding the stout and comfortable figure above her.

"All heaven, and you're spoiling me!" she observed.

"But certainly no porridge . . . As it seems I've got the morning off, I'm going to be lazy!"

"And a good thing too, after all that fuss yesterday!" Mrs. Brathay sniffed. "I was going to leave you a nice warm supper in the oven, but Tim said you'd get something at the doctor's. Which I suppose you did?"

"Yes." Hilary wished she could control that annoying inexplicable tendency to colour up. "Mrs. Tyson looked after us splendidly."

"Ah, she would." Cousin Priscilla stated the fact without rancour. "A nice old lady, that – one of the real old school. His nannie, wasn't she? Easy to see she's devoted to him." She gave Hilary a sudden, piercing look. "Knows what's good for him – and that includes you, my dear!"

"What can you mean?" Hilary laughed, keeping her eyes on the laden breakfast tray on her knees.

"Well, everyone knows how good you are at your job," Cousin Priscilla went on with her usual devastating frankness. "It's always the same when a man's good-looking – he gets what he wants and there's an end of it!"

There was a moment's silence. Then:

"I hope," Hilary told her rather stiffly, "that my capabilities would never depend on my employer's looks, handsome or otherwise. No doubt if I were seventeen it might be so. But as it is—"

"As it is, you could be just as capable if he were eighty – Oh, of course!" Cousin Priscilla pursed her lips, a sudden mischievous light in her grey-blue eyes. "I'm quite sure of that, my dear. Well, we won't quarrel over obvious facts. Now finish your orange juice and don't let the eggs go cold. You need rest after all that to-do yesterday. A mercy no one was killed."

Suppressing a desire to argue with her cousin's earlier remarks and assure her she could not be more wrong in her assumptions, Hilary said:

"I'm not in the least tired after such a long lie-in. I think I'll go along to see how Frant is. She and John Dallam were towers of strength yesterday."

"I'm sure they were," Cousin Priscilla agreed, going to the door. "Plain to see how the land lies in *that* direction! John is mighty taken with Miss Frant, and I've a notion she's not entirely indifferent to him, for all her teasing when he's around."

She went out shutting the door firmly, and left Hilary to finish her scrambled eggs and drink some excellent coffee, poised between laughter and irritation. Really, Cousin Priscilla was incorrigible; a born romantic with a penchant for matchmaking that could sometimes be quite blatant!

But while she idly flipped through the pages of the newspaper which had been brought up on her tray, the memory of last night came back with surprising vividness, interposing itself between her and the contents of the printed page; and with that memory came a man's tired face smiling at her in the dim light, the clasp of firm fingers about her own, and the echo of his voice – that undoubtedly very attractice voice, saying:

"Thank you – a thousand times . . . You've been – more than a tower of strength . . . I may seem to take things for granted, but I'm not ungrateful for very valuable services rendered. Thank you, Hilary."

Foolish, how her heart had quickened when he called her by her Christian name for the first time! Even more foolish to feel that same flutter of pulses now—

She thrust the paper from her impatiently and throwing back the bedclothes, stepped into her slippers and picked up her dressing-gown. Half an hour later, a hot bath having taken away the last lingering aches from yesterday's exertions, she was dressed and ready to go out.

As she went downstairs old Shep the Border collie, now retired from a long and honourable career to settle down as a domestic patriarch, padded gravely into the hall from the kitchen, and intimated that he would like to accompany her out. But patting his greying head, she told him:

"Not this morning, old boy. Frant may be working, and you'd get bored and fidget. Stay and keep Jenks company." Jenks the large black and white cat, who had also emerged, but from the sitting-room, uttered a throaty mew and curled round her legs. Originally employed to keep down rats and mice, he had become too well-fed to bother with such menial tasks, and left them to a couple of younger cats with more energy. Now, sitting and regarding his mistress with an unblinking stare, he was not unlike a portly alderman in full evening dress. He condescended to accompany Hilary to the gate, Shep beside them. Then losing interest he sat down in the middle of the garden path and started to shampoo himself, while the collie gazed somewhat reproachfully through the iron-work of the gate as Hilary set off for the village.

Cousin Priscilla leaned from an upper window, and waving a duster, called goodbye, while at the top of a field above the house Hilary glimpsed the distant figure of her brother talking to two of his men. Willowbeck Farm was ticking over to the time of early spring, as it had done for centuries; and it was in a mood of quiet content that she turned and walked down towards the bridge over the beck.

Last night's storm had blown itself out and the valley was brilliant with pale sunshine from a sky of robin's egg blue across which feathery clouds scudded under a fresh breeze. As usual yellow wagtails were busy about their business of nesting-time along by the beck, hazel and hawthorn were in budding leaf, and amid the gold sallies of catkins a robin sang gaily, a very different theme from his thin little winter tune, while he was answered by a blackbird perched on a burgeoning willow, his own bill golden in the sun. There were mauve and white crocuses in the cottage gardens she passed, and the first daffodils nodding trumpets among the vivid blue of scillas. She felt her spirits lifting with the bright morning and sang softly to herself while she passed through the village, which at this hour seemed to be deserted, save for a few shoppers who called smiling greetings. Turning off down the road past the church that led to Frant's house, she slowed her pace outside the windows of John Dallam's shop. The door was open, and to her surprise Frant herself came out, looking worried and rather harassed.

"Hullo, what are you doing here? I was just on my way to see you," Hilary greeted her, and then: "Anything wrong?"

"Well, slightly. This first-class idiot—" Frant gestured into the dusky interior of the shop, "was on a stepladder mending up the broken top of an Adam dresser when he slipped and ripped his arm on a six-inch nail. I happened to be passing and looked into find him weltering in gore and saying it was only a scratch! I've telephoned for your boss, who I trust is on his way now. I tried all my best first aid, but he's still bleeding like a pig."

"Darling Frant, don't fuss!" John emerged from the back premises, a hand held to an alarmingly scarlet bandage on his left arm, his face rather pale but a wry grin on his pleasantly ugly features. "I always bleed like a pig if a pin touches me – nothing to worry about."

"Sit down at once and let me see to that," Hilary ordered, taking in the situation at a glance. "Wait, and I'll apply a tourniquet. Frant, fetch me hot water and boracic. This will have to be stitched—"

"Oo – er! I'm not going to die, am I, Nurse?" John enquired, reclining in a genuine Windsor chair. "Do say I am, because then maybe Frant will take pity on me and allow a deathbed marriage to be performed – and every year on the anniversary she can come and weep over the snowdrops on my grave and repent of her cruelty to me."

"Silly ass!" said Frant heartlessly, going to obey her friend's instructions, while Hilary commanded:

"Don't move that arm! The sooner Bla – Dr. Kinross sees it, the better. But I'm afraid he won't be around at present—" She stopped when as if on a cue a familiar voice demanded from the open doorway:

"What's going on here? What have you been doing to yourself, young Dallam?"

"Hullo, Doc! You perceive me in the hands of two ministering angels – but if you want to save me while there's time, just prescribe a large brandy and soda!" John told the newcomer.

By now Hilary had applied a makeshift tourniquet of clean linen and a pencil which had been conveniently near. As Frant came in with a renewed enamel bowl of hot water, Blake, bending over the patient, gave an approving nod.

"Keep still," he ordered. "We'll get this stitched up right away." Opening his case, he glanced at Hilary, frowning slightly. "I thought you were to take the morning off?"

"I was just passing – this was supposed to be a social call," she told him. "At least I was on my way to Frant, but I found her here."

"Which was the merest chance," Frant broke in rather quickly, her cheeks slightly pink. "I'd come to find out if this clumsy idiot had any news of that poor bus driver and the others who had to go to hospital yesterday – only to find he was trying to make a hospital case of his silly self!"

"Frant, my sweet – always so feminine and soothing!" John murmured, leaning back his eyes closed. "Couldn't you make a painting of this – 'The Wounded Warrior After Waterloo'? With me in gallant scarlet, you and Hilary in demure dresses, and the Doc in sombre black and a top hat . . . Ouch!"

"Keep quiet and don't wriggle!" Blake told him. "How

56

did you do this – fall on an antique dagger or merely an outsize nail?"

"The latter," John replied. "I – oh, lor," he added in a lower tone. "Customers! Keep them away from this gory scene, you girls, or they'll fly the premises with loud shrieks."

"There's only one," Frant returned. "I'll try to head her off if she comes in as far as this." She moved away, and Hilary who was holding the bowl of water, her eyes on the doctor's deft fingers, asked, her own voice lowered:

"How is the driver today – and the others who had to be detained?"

"The driver's not too bad, but won't be out for some weeks, poor fellow," Blake answered. "Two of the others have been sent home to take things quietly, and those still in hospital will be out in a few days. It was little short of a miracle that that accident had no worse consequences."

"Indeed it was," Hilary agreed fervently, and as Frant's and a husky, rather drawling girl's voice came nearer, looked round. "Oh dear! I'd better mop up, or John will certainly lose a customer."

"Go ahead, then." Blake, who had finished stitching his patient's arm and was now fastening a bandage, looked up with a smile. "And remove that basin. As for you, young Dallam—"

"I wish you wouldn't call me that," John said plaintively. "You remind me of a prefect at my school, about to make me extremely sore where I sit down—"

"Which you no doubt deserved," Blake laughed. "But all *I* am telling you is to take that sore arm upstairs and lie down for a bit. At lunch time you may have the brandy and soda of which you spoke so feelingly earlier!"

"Bless your kind heart, Dr. Kinross!" Still very pale, John sat up and grinned at his benefactor. "I'll obey your orders – and if the lady with whom Frant seems to be holding an animated conversation offers to buy my entire

57

stock for thirty thousand pounds, I'll treat you all to a cake for tea!"

He got to his feet, and with slightly unsteady steps made his way to the back premises, protesting as Blake, a firm hand on his sound arm, accompanied him up the stairs which led to the young man's living quarters.

Hilary glanced after them, a half-smile on her lips. But in her heart and mind she was aware of a conflicting surge of emotions, out of which no one feeling was at that moment able to emerge clearly. Trained in medical discipline herself, she was at a loss to know what impressed her most – the light skill of those expert hands, the way he could establish that casual yet so infinitely important rapport with his patient, be it a young man or an elderly and frightened woman – or a man in imminent danger of death as the driver of that bus could so easily have been yesterday, when the doctor had climbed through tangled wreckage to administer comfort and healing . . .

She came back to earth with a little start, realising that Frant and the apparently prospective customer were talking somewhere quite near. Hurriedly picking up the basin, she carried it through to the scullery that led off the kitchen at the back, and then returning into the shop was joined by Blake.

Before they could exchange a word Frant came towards them accompanied by a tall, slender figure, a fair-haired girl in a perfectly cut tweed suit, her heart shaped face framed by an aureole of natural curls. Hilary was aware of pale, greenish-blue eyes of an unusual but fascinating hue under arched gold brows. A beautiful face marred by an arrogant hauteur of expression, and the discontented mouth of a spoilt woman. The face of the girl in the car yesterday.

". . . So madly interesting!" the newcomer was saying to Frant, who was wearing what Hilary instantly recognised as the "polite" expression, which meant that she was not

58

liking her companion. "But of course even more interesting for my husband Vernon, who comes from this part of the world. That's why he's bought Hollins Hall – it became an absolute *obsession* with him when he heard it was up for sale. He went all Lakeland dalesman, and prosed on about roots in the land and forebears and all that sort of thing! Never having given anything of the sort for decades, if you ask me! But we shall only spend a part of each year up here, naturally. Vernon has so many other interests, and we seem to be simply cluttered up with houses all over the world. We've just come from our little place in Jamaica, I do hope that doesn't sound horribly ostentatious, but—"

Becoming aware of Blake with Hilary standing beside him in the slightly shadowy recess at the back of the shop, she broke off abruptly. Then:

"*Blake!* Good heavens, it can't be true! What in the name of all that's wonderful are you doing here?"

As he took the slender hand extended to him, Blake's smile was set and a little bleak. "I might ask the same of yourself," he returned coolly. "I should have hardly thought this rural part of the world would have had any appeal to you, Lena."

Was there just the faintest ring of sarcasm in that rejoinder? Looking from one to the other Hilary was aware that the two of them had received a mutual and far from pleasant shock. Her second thought came with an odd pang: That she had seldom seen anyone lovelier.

But it was a loveliness marred by lips that were ungenerously thin under their skilfully applied make-up, and all Hilary's experience of human nature gained in a big hospital told her that here was the kind of selfish egotism that would always take without giving. Hard as nails under that glowing mask, and yet with a power to enslave men, and leave indelible scars on those who lost their hearts to her.

59

Had there been a time when Blake cared? Just how well did these two know each other, for this encounter to cause such obvious tension? And what is that to do with me? Hilary asked herself.

Blake's sherry-coloured eyes were still bleak as he went on, "Let me see – you're Mrs. Fairfax now, aren't you? Tarnmere is surely very far removed from your usual more exotic settings."

Her laugh was a little brittle. "I suppose you see those awful pictures from time to time in the glossy illustrateds: 'Mrs. Vernon Fairfax with friends on the terrace of her château' – the usual revolting and unwanted bits of publicity. But I insist on knowing what you're up to in the English lakes?"

"Nothing very exciting. I'm the local doctor here."

"*No!* I'm knocked sideways!"

"Are you? I don't see why."

"But my dear! I thought you were all set for a brass plate in Harley Street, in spite of the fact that you so often denied any such ambition! But what on earth made you bury yourself in the dales of Lakeland?"

"Inclination," he said coolly. "I've returned to the country of my forebears."

"How madly romantic! And do you like it?"

"If I didn't I shouldn't be here."

"That I can believe. You were always inclined to do exactly what you wanted, weren't you?"

"Perhaps I was – within the limits of my profession."

"Ah, yes, of course – your profession." There was a sudden sarcastic ring to those clear tones. "It always came first with you, if I remember rightly."

Blake smiled, and glancing from his set face to the vivid features of the girl who stood directly in front of him, Hilary was again conscious of that breathless tension in the air – rather as if two fencers were parrying blades in the preliminary to a duel. There was a cold indifference on the part of the man, a sophisticated but slightly shrill defence where the girl was concerned. And beneath – something deeper, something that ran swiftly between them like the surging waters of an underground river with eddying currents, both deep and treacherous.

As if aware of her companion's silence and resenting it, the girl in the tweed suit said, still in those slightly high-pitched tones:

"Am I right in supposing you must have been on that extremely dreary hillside last night in all that mud and rain? We offered help, but it didn't seem to be wanted."

"It was extremely kind of you, but luckily by that time the crisis was safely over. Mercifully, there were no fatalities." Blake's answer held a quiet courtesy that the other seemed to find slightly daunting, and there was a brief silence. Then:

"I'm so glad. Vernon was ready to do anything he could to help. His mother came from this part of the world, you know, and so he feels himself as at least partly belonging to Lakeland. And he's crazy on climbing these awful mountains! That's one of the reasons he snapped up Hollins Hall when he heard it was up for sale." She paused, and as Blake still said nothing: "Surely you remember Vernon? He was," her laugh was meant to be natural and yet somehow only succeeded in sounding a little strained, "always the most determined of my suitors."

"I remember him very well," said Blake evenly, and changing the subject with some abruptness: "I see you've already met Miss Frant. Let me introduce Miss Talgarth – my secretary. Mrs. Fairfax, Hilary."

"How do you do?" Lena Fairfax nodded briefly, and was turning towards Frant when the shop door was pushed open and the rather bulky figure of the man Hilary had seen in the Rolls last night came in.

"I thought I might find you here, Lena," he said. "But I rather doubt—" his hard grey glance round the shop's interior was faintly disparaging, "if you'll find anything worth while in village dealers in these days. Tourists aided by television programmes have sent prices rocketing and quality down. Local sales are more likely to bring you the old oak you say you want for the dining room."

"Vernon darling – always so right where getting a bargain is concerned," Lena returned, the faintest note of sarcasm in her light tones. "But for once I have an idea you're going to be wrong. I've already spotted the most enchanting little bow-fronted walnut lowboy; and if it isn't too restored I intend to have it. But my dear, such a delightful and unexpected surprise – just look who I've found from the old days in London. No less a person than Blake Kinross, who's the doctor here – surely you two must remember each other?"

Nothing could have been sweeter than her smiling gesture towards Blake who, case in hand, was about to leave. Vernon Fairfax, who had not yet glanced his way, gave a very perceptible start, and for a moment the two men regarded each other in dead silence.

Aware of sudden, almost electric tension, Hilary glanced from one to the other: Blake, tall and lean and dark, so very good to look at, but with that almost cold remote look which told her he was anything but pleased at this encounter; and the big-shouldered, burly greyhaired man with a square, not unhandsome face whose formidable jaw, and eyes the colour of granite matched a mouth at once uncompromising and with a hint of sensuality kept in iron control; the mouth of a man of strong passions, and even stronger temper when roused. A man not without attraction for many women (apart from his enormous wealth!) and who might be near his sixties, yet carried his years with an arrogant ease befitting a much younger male.

Vernon Fairfax might have "big business" written large in his personality, but there was something formidable, even, Hilary thought, a little frightening about his strong personality that set him apart from others of his stamp whom she had previously encountered. Money and power, and a fierce pride of possession; did his wife, so much younger, so supremely sure of herself, realise just the type of man she had married? Looking at that golden beauty, smiling and indulgent, but with little of awareness apart from her own attractions, Hilary rather doubted it.

The silence, which suddenly threatened to become embarrassing, was broken by Blake saying easily: "How are you, Fairfax? It's quite a time since we met."

"It is indeed. And so you're the doctor here." Vernon Fairfax's tone was indifferent, matching Blake's, and he did not attempt to offer a hand. "You must have had a busy day yesterday, judging from what I saw when we passed that wrecked bus. Any fatalities?"

"Fortunately, no. A few injured, but none seriously except for the driver, poor fellow, and he'll soon be on the mend." Blake's tone was impersonally courteous. "And now if you'll forgive me I must be getting along," He glanced at Hilary, and for the first time that morning the warm smile which so transformed his face appeared. "Tell young Dallam from me to take things easy for today, and I'll look in on him tomorrow. Meanwhile, give him a little longer, and then you'd better inform him that he has some potential custom. See you this afternoon."

Then with a courteous nod that took in the assembled company he went out to his car. To her annoyance Hilary knew that her colour had deepened under the sudden warmth in his eyes, a fact that had not escaped Lena Fairfax. If that sophisticated lady's eyes had sharpened into a momentary flash of annoyance, it was no longer evident as she said lightly:

"I suppose Blake leads a terribly busy life, Miss – I didn't quite catch your name?"

"Hilary Talgarth. I'm Dr. Kinross's secretary," Hilary reminded her evenly.

"Oh, yes, of course," Lena drawled. "I—" She broke off, raising her brows as she saw her husband staring at Miss Talgarth, sudden interest in his eyes.

"Hilary Talgarth?" he asked. "Was your grandfather Jonathan Talgarth of Willowbeck Farm?"

"Yes." Hilary looked at him in surprise, which deepened as he stepped across to her, and his hard face softened, held out his hand. "My father and old Jonathan were great friends when I was only so high," he told her. "And I'm delighted to meet his – if I may say so – extremely ornamental granddaughter! I was born over the Raise, you know – or more likely don't!" He laughed. "This is something of a sentimental journey back to where my roots lie. Also, I'm very keen on climbing, and though I'm told I'm getting past it (which I certainly am where the really high peaks are concerned), I'm determined to try some of the easier ascents when I can spare the time."

"Are you making your home here for good, then?" Hilary asked, returning the warmth of his clasp.

He shook his head. "I've still too much travelling around for that; but Hollins Hall will certainly remain mine – to come back to when I'm able. I'm afraid my wife would soon fade away from boredom if she was asked to stay up here for very long. But we're certainly going to settle in for a time."

Hilary could not help wondering afresh at the coldness he had shown towards Blake Kinross and his attitude to herself. It was obvious that his pleasure was not shared by his wife, who said lightly:

"So you work for the doctor – how very interesting that must be. But do tell me – what was he doing here? Is someone ill in the place?"

"No, but Mr. Dallam, the owner of this business, had a slight accident – a rather nasty cut. We—" She glanced at

Frant, who had moved to the staircase at the back of the shop and was standing with her back to the Fairfaxes. For some reason she apparently did not want to get into conversation with either of them. "We're only a couple of friends who happened to be passing by when John – Mr. Dallam – had a fall and needed help," she continued. "He'll be down very shortly, so meanwhile if you want to look round—"

"Oh, that would be fine. Don't disturb him on our account," Lena answered. "Come over here, Vernon darling, and tell me if I'm not right about this piece. Such a charming lowboy, and I believe the handles are original."

"They seem to be. And the back is O.K." Her husband was already standing over the bow-fronted lowboy whose exquisitely proportioned lines and mellow gold patina of delicately-grained walnut proclaimed it as Queene Anne or very early Georgian. Hilary knew that John had picked it up in the sale of the contents of a big house in a lonely part of the dales on a rainy day when big dealers had been few; it was one of the finest pieces he had ever discovered, and having had it on his hands for some months, he had more than once announced that he could hardly bear the idea of parting with it!

"Certainly not under a handsome sum," Frant had admonished; and now, pulling a quick face at Hilary, she went softly and unobtrusively upstairs. There Hilary could hear a muted exchange of conversation which was counterblanced by an equally low-toned colloquy between the Fairfaxes of which she caught snatches.

"Drawers O.K. Handles original, and no chips in the veneer." Vernon Fairfax was on his knees and turned up the cabriolet feet with a gentleness that yet belied muscular strength. "No sign of worm either . . . Can't think how it ever came to be in a shop like this . . . Wonder if the man realises just what he's got hold of?"

"I adore it!" Lena announced. "In spite of the fact that

what I was actually looking for is genuine Tudor oak! I don't care what the price is." She lowered her voice at an upward scowl from her husband, still kneeling beside the lowboy. "Well, I don't! Just think what it would fetch in a London saleroom!"

"That's just it," Fairfax answered sharply. "It wouldn't be a penny under—" Hilary could not catch the figure he named, but she heard the admonition: "Not a penny beyond four hundred – and we ought to get less than that—"

Neither of them had noticed Frant's disappearance up the stairs, or her descent a few moments later. Hilary, seeing a notepad and pencil on a small table beside her, picked it up, scribbled a brief line unnoticed by the others. She was looked at in surprise by Frant, who opened her mouth but was imperatively scowled into silence.

"Before I go, I'll just let Mr. Dallam know you're here," Hilary said brightly, and brushing past her friend, went lightly up the stairs. At the top she met John, still pale but looking considerably better for his rest.

Seeing Hilary he paused in astonishment. "What – ?" he began, but was shushed into silence while she said loudly:

"You've got customers, John, so you'd better come down now. Frant and I must be getting along—" At the same instant she pushed the folded paper she held into his hand and whispered: "Read that!" And without giving him time to answer, she descended into the shop again. "Mr. Dallam will be down in a minute," she announced. "Good afternoon." And with a smile at the Fairfaxes who were both too occupied to do more than absently return her farewell she left, followed by her friend.

Meanwhile, half way down the stairs, John had clumsily unfolded the paper so hastily shoved into his surprised grasp, and read:

"The lowboy is worth far more than we thought. Start bargain-

ing at four-fifty, but don't dare come down more than the odd bit."

John read it twice, gave a gulp, crumpled the paper into his pocket, and descended to do battle.

"I can't say I take much to the newest 'offcomes' to the village," Frant remarked as they walked down the winding road between banks of early celandine and an occasional early primrose towards her house by the lake. "Stinking rich, of course, and on the part of the lady, madly spoiled. She's very pleased with herself and very sure of her tycoon husband – but I trust for her own sake she doesn't get too sure. I know that Power Game type, and I'll lay my last groat he's got the devil's own temper coiled deep down under that rather heavy exterior. Quite handsome in his way, I suppose. They obviously mean to buy John's precious lowboy, so I hope he's got the sense to get a really good price . . . What are you grinning about?"

"He will," Hilary assured her, and told her about the note she had gone up to give John.

Frant threw back her head and uttered her delightful laugh. "Darling Hilary, good for you!" she exclaimed. "Stay to lunch before you go back to your work, and no doubt we'll find out how the bargaining has gone."

Hilary accepted the invitation with pleasure, but long before lunch was due to be served a tall figure, one arm interestingly in a sling, the other holding a carrier, appeared up the garden path. It was John, and from his beaming face his story was told before Frant had opened the front door and greeted:

"Don't tell us! The password is Success!"

"And good fortune!" In his exuberance John kissed them both – Frant resoundingly, Hilary on the cheek. "What it is to have good friends! How did you guess, Hilary?"

"Did you get the four hundred?" she demanded.

"I did! Not without a deuce of a lot of bargaining, but he paid up in the end – his lady wife wouldn't have let him get out of it in any case. Gosh, when that one wants a thing she sees, she gets it!" John laughed. "But this I must know – *how* did you know what to ask, Hilary?" And when she explained: "But what quick thinking! I wasn't going to ask a penny over two-fifty, or three hundred at the outside. Evidently it's time I pulled up my nylon socks!"

"Of course it is! I always said you were a goof and too soft to be in the antique trade, especially in these antique-mad times," Frant told him. "If that's champagne you're carrying, it must wait until tonight! I'll cook an extra special dinner with my own lily-white hands, and we'll all get madly tipsy."

"Oh!" Her beloved looked somewhat dashed. "I thought we'd kill a couple of bottles of Veuve Cliquot now, and hang the time of day—"

"John Dallam! You're nothing less than a dissolute seducer of innocent young females in the middle of a spring afternoon!" His beloved's horrified accent was belied by the glint in her eyes. "Do you want to lose Miss Talgarth her impeccable task of aiding Dr. Kinross? Do you want me to ruin my reputation by causing me to paint an indubitable copy of Graham Sutherland's Helena Rubinstein which will at once destroy my reputation for ever as a miserable plagiarist? Your champagne will go straight – not to our heads, but into the bottom of the fridge where it will remain until a respectable hour this evening."

"As you say, Frant darling." John meekly surrendered his offering. "I will remain sober – but I warn you, I shall expect a dinner worthy of Escoffier at eight-thirty prompt this evening."

"Well, you won't get it," Frant retorted. "It's Mrs. Elleray's night off, and you'll have to put up with a *dîner à la Frant*. Which means you won't starve, and your champagne shall be done justice to. More I won't promise."

But in spite of her somewhat blighting promise, the dinner served that evening was more than worthy of the wine – from the prawn cocktail with a very special dressing, to the *caneton à l'orange* through to a pineapple soufflé with just the right aromatic tang to counteract any possible richness, all was perfection. Congratulated on her culinary powers, Frant briefly confessed to having learned more than painting during a sojourn in Paris, having shared digs on the Left Bank with a certain Cécile who was studying for her *cordon bleu*.

But it was over liqueurs that John observed: "It seemed to me that the lowboy wasn't the only subject Mrs. Fairfax was interested in this afternoon. She seemed very taken with the fact that our doctor was once quite a friend of hers in London." He chuckled. "She kept on asking me questions about him – said that she was sure he must have some time for social life, and of course they must have him in for a drink, mustn't they, Vernon darling? Vernon darling looked like a thundercloud, and so obviously hates Kinross's guts – to put it vulgarly – that having a murky mind I couldn't help concluding that the doc must be an old flame of hers. So I suppose it's hardly surprising that warm remembrance of things past didn't strike any answering spark in the doctor's breast, any more than her reminiscences gave her husband the slightest pleasure." He paused, swirling the amber liquid round his glass. "Also, I couldn't help hearing some of what was being said earlier, while I was up in my room. I must say an iceberg would have been warm in comparison with Kinross's reception of her renewed acquaintance."

"Yes, it was very obvious he didn't want to be reminded of anything there may have been in the past," Frant agreed rather quickly, glancing at Hilary who, keeping her eyes on her own glass, was quite silent.

"Bit intriguing, eh?" John went on cheerfully. "Maybe

he had his young life blighted by her – though I shouldn't have thought she was ever his type. But—"

"John dear, whatever may have happened is really none of our business," Frant said somewhat impatiently. And as John glanced at her, surprised and a little hurt by the snub, his beloved flickered a warning glance towards Hilary. John reddened, and taking the hint, said in some haste:

"You couldn't be more right, sweetie. Anyway, it's obvious he couldn't care less – though I should think Fairfax is the type who's easily jealous of his wife even when he has no reason to be." Then deftly changing the subject, "Odd, the way he's come back to the dales. His wife says it's because he was born near here, and is keen on climbing, but I shouldn't have thought he had an ounce of sentiment in his make-up. Though I suppose even the toughest tycoon has soft chinks in his armour."

"No doubt," Frant agreed drily. "But I should think both your rich customers will be bored stiff with Tarn-mere in a couple of months at the most; and if they start to throw their weight about in the village, they'll very soon learn that that sort of thing doesn't go down well with the dalesfolk."

"But don't forget what you've just said – that so far as Vernon Fairfax is concerned he's a returned native," said Hilary.

"So he is. That possibly makes it different,' Frant agreed.

But just how different none of them guessed.

CHAPTER FIVE

SEATED at her desk, her fingers busy with the typewriter while she dealt with a pile of correspondence, Hilary was annoyed and impatient with herself to find how often there rose between the work before her the picture of Lena Fairfax's face.

And as the memory came unbidden, so there recurred the unwelcome question which, she told herself angrily, she had no right to ask: just what part had young Mrs. Fairfax played in Blake Kinross's life in those past days – over three years now – when he had been a promising houseman at St. Ethelreda's Hospital in the heart of London.

Somehow the mere idea of Blake ever having been seriously interested in someone so obviously spoiled and self-centred as Lena Fairfax must always have been was curiously distasteful. Hilary could not imagine Blake, even as a much younger man, mixing in the sort of fashionable, shallow set of which she guessed the other girl must have been the centre.

Well! It was very obvious – as John Dallam had remarked – that whatever there had been between those two, the reappearance of Lena Fairfax in his life was anything but welcome. Yet wasn't it equally obvious that Lena, married to wealth and power in the formidable shape of her older husband, was far from without interest on coming into contact with this particular person from her past?

Finding the question more than usually unpalatable, Hilary bit her lip, and turning her attention to the letter beside her machine, banged the keys with more than usual force. She was immersed in work when a tap at the door made her glance up with slight impatience and call, "Come in!"

The door opened and Mrs. Tyson entered, bearing a tray with a cup of tea and a slice of cake.

"You've been working for an age and it's long past tea-time," she said reprovingly. "I didn't like to disturb you before. Dr. Blake should be back from Windermere any time now, but as I knew you had a lot to do I let you work on. But now it's high time for a nice hot cup of tea."

"Good heavens, is it five already?" Hilary glanced at her wrist-watch. "Well, I got in late from lunch, and there's still another half hour's work or more. But thank you for the tea, it's most welcome, Mrs. Tyson."

"Wouldn't you like a paste sandwich, or some currant pasty?" the housekeeper asked coaxingly. "I know you never take much at this time, but—"

"No, thanks," Hilary shook her head, smiling affectionately at her companion. And then, her glance falling on her plate beside the tea-cup: "Why, what's this? Your own gingerbread – lovely!"

"Well, eat up and enjoy it!" Mrs. Tyson admonished. She turned to the door, and then after a moment's hesitation remained where she was, her hands pleating the folds of the spotless white apron that adorned her small, trim form. "I've been busy most of the afternoon making cakes and biscuits – it's a thing I always find soothing when I'm put about or worried."

"Is something worrying you?" Hilary glanced across at her in surprise and some concern as she saw the shadow on the housekeeper's face, worn with the wrinkles of a lifetime's caring for others. "Yes, I see there is. What's wrong? Or can't I help?"

"Not help, dear." Mrs. Tyson took the chair Hilary indicated, and looking at her young companion with trouble in her faded eyes, blurted out: "It's Master Blake

72

— I mean, the doctor — but you won't breathe a word of what I say, will you?"

"Of course not." Hilary felt her heart miss a beat. "Why should you be worried about the doctor? There's — nothing wrong with him, surely?"

"Not at the moment, but that's not to say there won't be," Mrs. Tyson returned ominously. "To think that such a thing should happen here in Tarnmere of all places in the world! The one bit of the whole globe where I'd have been ready to swear he would never set eyes on her again. And now—"

"What do you mean, Mrs. Tyson?" Hilary was about to pick up her cup, but set it down in its saucer, her eyes on the housekeeper's anxious face. She felt sure she knew the answer before, after a moment's further hesitation, Mrs. Tyson said angrily:

"That Mrs. Vernon Fairfax as she now is — Lena Weston that was, when she was a leader of that smart set down in London years back. Her father was someone very important on the hospital board, and the doctor and that girl met socially, and in no time she'd scooped him up and added him to her admirers — who were already many enough, dear knows. She was always a beauty, though ice-cold under that warm pretty manner she knew how to put on so well! Hard as iron, too, as the poor boy — for he *was* only a boy then, for all his cleverness and getting on in his profession — found out soon enough when she finally let him down flat because she realised he wasn't ambitious to be a fashionable doctor. No country practice for *her* husband!"

Gazing into the past, her hands working on her apron, it seemed that Mrs. Tyson had forgotten her listener, forgotten her surroundings, and her faded eyes, usually so kindly, were hard with anger. "When the rich Mr. Vernon Fairfax with his huge fortune came along she never hesitated about taking him — in spite of the fact that she had

73

become engaged to Master Blake only two months previously!"

"Engaged?" Hilary felt as though something hard had hit her directly over the region of her heart. Her voice sounded suddenly loud in her own ears and the housekeeper, jerked out of her memories, looked across, startled at her pallor.

"Maybe I shouldn't have spoken – but I'm so upset I just felt I had to speak to someone," she said. "It was the biggest shock I've ever had in years when I saw her in the village today – and I heard about how she'd bought some valuable furniture from young Mr. Dallam. It seems that you've already met her, Miss Hilary, so you can judge for yourself whether I'm not right to worry."

"But—" Hilary paused, at a loss for words. It was far from surprising that the morning's happenings at John Dallam's were already a juicy titbit for the village to mull over gleefully along with the Fairfaxes' arrival at Hollins Hall. After a moment she went on: "I'll admit that I – didn't exactly take to the lady, but I think you're worrying over something that couldn't possibly matter any longer, Mrs. Tyson. Even if – if Mrs. Fairfax and the doctor were once engaged and she threw him over, that all lies in the past. Dr. Kinross, is I'm certain, the last person in the world to let anything like that cause him a moment's worry now. And from what I can gather Mrs. Fairfax won't be staying here for long at a time – the buying of the house is just a rich man's whim. He bought it for sentimental reasons, because some of his roots lie in this part of the world, and he wants to do some climbing, evidently of old familiar places he knew in his youth. But they'll soon be off again, what with his evidently very big business interests all over the world, and the fact that his wife would very soon become bored to tears with life up here. And in the meantime she and the doctor are only likely to meet in the most occasional and casual fashion."

74

(That, she hoped, was true. But the unwelcome thought intruded: *How, perhaps, were those meetings going to affect him?*)

The housekeeper sighed and rose from her chair. "I hope you're right, Miss Hilary," she replied. "Only I've a strong feeling it won't all work out as easy as that—"

"But, dear Mrs. Tyson, what do you mean?" Hilary comforted, trying to sound convinced. "There's nothing to 'work out'. Mrs. Fairfax, however badly she may have behaved in the past, is now married and has everything in the world a person of her type can possibly want. Besides, I'm sure the doctor would never—"

"Oh, it's not the doctor I'm afraid of," said Nannie Tyson quickly. "You may say I'm a daft old fool, but I've a feeling about that Lena. She's a troublemaker, and my fear is that she'll bring him trouble."

"But how could she possibly do so?"

"Ah!" The housekeeper shook her head. "I don't feel I'm making a fuss about nowt, however it may look to you, my dear. You see, I know her so well from those old days when Dr. Blake was so much in love with her, and so wildly happy in their engagement. And she's the type who'd never change – a cruel cat of a girl. And only I know how desperately unhappy she made him. He's got over it, and then she's got to come back into his life and remind him of it all; and mark my words, she's untrustworthy, cunning and selfish to the core! Maybe I'm just a stupid old woman, but all my life I've had hunches – I'm half Highland, you know – and I'm not happy. After she jilted him he never looked at another girl. If only he'd met the right one and was safely married I'd feel happier."

She paused, her eyes suddenly misty. "He only opened out to me once, on the evening after she broke the engagement. Then he said—" Her voice quavered as she impatiently brushed a hand over her eyes: " 'Nannie,' he

75

said, 'we all have to buy our experience, and I've just bought mine with the bitterness of knowing just how big a fool love can make a man. I gave her my heart – I'd have given her the rest of my life – and all the time she was shut away in her own shallow world. I love a mirage, and it's completely faded. If you ever catch me beginning to make such a fool of myself again, warn me with just one word – the one King Charles I uttered when he was about to lose his head physically as I lost mine in a less literal sense!' And when I asked him what that word was, he said: '*Remember!* Just say that, and I'll come to my senses in double quick time.' He laughed as he said it, but such a laugh – of bitterness and misery. I could have killed her then, and I still don't feel much more kindly to her now . . . Oh, I wish with all my heart and soul they hadn't met again!"

Compelled against her will to ask the questions, Hilary said: "And have you ever had to give him that – warning?"

"Never!" Mrs. Tyson retorted emphatically. "From that day to this he's never so much as looked at another girl. Soon after he was offered a post in an Edinburgh hospital, and he worked there until he came to Tarndale. He's lived for his work ever since, but he's been a very lonely man." She smoothed her apron with hands that were suddenly no longer unsteady. "I've been talking far too much. Forgive me. I know I can trust you never to repeat a word, and it's been a help to have someone to confide in."

"I'm glad. And of course I'll respect your confidence, Mrs. Tyson." With something of an effort Hilary smiled at her. "Please don't go on worrying and fretting yourself – I'm sure there's no need to."

The housekeeper shook her head again. "I wish I could be sure of that. Well, I must get on, or his dinner won't be ready."

And with a worried sigh she turned and left the room,

76

shutting the door quietly behind her. For some minutes Hilary sat very still, staring in front of her, letting her second cup of tea grow cold, her eyes shadowed.

Mrs. Tyson's confidences had been unexpected, but need they have been quite so – shattering in their impact? she asked herself. She had been prepared to hear that Blake Kinross and Lena Fairfax had once meant something to each other – Lena's obvious amusement, her oblique hints of those days years ago in London, and Blake's reaction of ice-cold detachment had shown that clearly enough. She understood the shock she had sensed last night only too well now. But had he ever truly forgotten the girl who had so ruthlessly shattered his dream of happiness?

Suddenly Hilary knew that she would rather not have been forced to hear Mrs. Tyson's unhappy confidences. To have the whole story flung at her out of the blue somehow sent everything awry. To have to meet him, as would happen at any moment now, knowing a story she had no right to know, and which if he suspected her knowledge, would certainly have angered him, filled her with embarrassment and dismay. She felt almost angry with the housekeeper until her innate sense of fairness told her that it was best to know, and so avoid possible pitfalls which might lie ahead in the immediate future.

For with Mrs. Tyson she was suddenly afraid that if Lena Fairfax's presence in Tarnmere did not spell deliberate trouble, the situation still held a possibility of complications. And it was Lena's husband of whom she was suddenly afraid. That big, ruthless man – for she was sure he was ruthless – adored his wife, and quite plainly he resented Blake. How stupid I am! she thought. He couldn't be jealous after all this time. After all, she married him!

"But she's a troublemaker." The housekeeper's words echoed back, but Hilary shrugged them aside with a fair

assumption of indifference. Well, what of it? Blake was surely capable of looking after himself.

But somehow the idea of his having been badly hurt by that elegant, self-assured woman she had encountered earlier filled Hilary with an anger the strength of which took her by surprise. It was not only the thought of all that that so much younger, more vulnerable Blake Kinross must have suffered; but the certainty that never, in whatever length of days were granted to her, would Lena Fairfax even begin to know the meaning of heartbreak or disillusion. Hilary, with her experienced nurse's acumen, had recognised the type the moment she set eyes on the other girl. Lena might suffer if her pride were ever touched; there was not one atom of warmth in her makeup, no feeling for anything but herself lay behind those deceptively smiling lips, those eyes which could open so invitingly when they looked into a man's; the only "love" she was capable of understanding was purely physical.

Certainly the last person in the world ever to have become a doctor's wife! How could the Blake Kinross she – Hilary – had known during these months in which they had worked together – coolly efficient, always so sure of himself, level-headed and inclined to be remote, ever have allowed himself to be ensnared by the sophisticated sexiness which Lena undoubtedly possessed, was something that puzzled and suddenly angered her. Not to have realised he was risking burnt wings at that flame – not to have been aware that to Lena the whole world was her golden oyster, to be opened and savoured to the full, was so alien to what Hilary knew of him that she became aware of a vague uneasiness which somehow while she worked on into the spring twilight, grew more definite.

While he had appeared supremely if politely indifferent to Lena, what had really been going on behind his more than usually sphinx-like façade? *Had* there been some reopening of old wounds, some chink opened in the armour with which he had so carefully encased his heart?

For after all, "there had never been another girl". Could not that be a sign that something of the old love lingered? Some faint glow amid the cold ashes which he had thought extinguished for ever? . . .

Hilary broke the thought abruptly, annoyed with herself for the sudden disturbance the thought brought – a vague unhappiness which she was resolute in not acknowledging. Still less was she ready to own that the new, desolate little pain nagging at her could be caused by memories of her own.

Very recent memories: of their working together during those hours of discomfort and cold and anxiety at the scene of that accident; of last night when in the very room leading off this one they had sat and talked, and let fall the sort of companionable silence that could only come from a mutual tiredness and – yes, contentment of a job done with mutual confidence that needed no words of after-discussion to enhance it. Last of all the memory of a firm clasp of strong fingers about her own, a smile that had warmed her heart, and words which had been with her on awakening today:

"... *You've been — more than a tower of strength . . . I'm not ungrateful for very valuable services rendered*" . . .

Oh, for goodness' sake! Must she keep on dwelling upon what had, at the very most, been no more than an expression of ordinary gratitude?

Impatiently she started on the last sheet of the pile of reports at which she had been working for so long, and finishing it ripped paper and carbon out of her machine almost viciously. She had just completed arranging the papers in a neat pile when a quick firm step sounded across the hall. A moment later the door opened, and Blake halted on the threshold.

"Hullo!" he exclaimed. "You still here?"

Could it be possible that there was something like

pleasure in the greeting? Almost before the thought set her heartbeats quickening, she noted the tiredness in his face, the deeply etched lines from nostril to lip, and a reflected weariness in his eyes that sent a swift, knife-like pain through her heart. He was working much too hard; too often at unrewarding, unnecessary things.

"I didn't realise it was so late. I wanted to get through the work which ought to have been done yesterday. We're all straight now. You're very late yourself," she said.

"There was a heck of a lot to see to at the hospital," he answered. "And as Matron was kind enough to ask me to an excellent tea, I couldn't get away before. You'll be glad to hear the patients are all doing fine – most of them will be able to go back to their homes tomorrow. And the driver is more comfortable, poor fellow, and very relieved to know that in a few weeks he'll be able to go back to his job."

"That's good anyway." She smiled at him, and going across put the cover on her typewriter. "Is there anything you'd like me to see to before I go home?"

"Nothing. You run along – unless," he added, glancing up from the top letter of the pile she had left ready for him, "you'd care to join me in an early sherry before going out into the cold?" And while she hesitated: "Come along! You're not going to tell me a modest glass, or even two, will topple you off your bike?"

They both laughed, and suddenly he looked less tired and the crease between his dark brows had gone.

"Very well. Thank you, I will," she agreed.

A few moments later, back in the room where they had dined last night, the warmth of firelight seemed to greet her with a welcoming glow that was suddenly reflected in her breast.

Blake asked, going across to a small table where a tray stood ready:

"How was John Dallam when you left him? That was a nasty cut."

"He was fine by the evening. He brought along a couple of bottles of champagne, if you please, and Frant cooked a really superb dinner – all to celebrate the fact that he sold that lowboy for a phenomenal sum. He was delighted, and seemed to have completely recovered."

"Ah, yes, I heard something about that. It must have been in the nature of a quite phenomenal tonic." Blake's tone was suddenly dry, and glancing up she saw his gaze was on the depths of the amber wine in the cut crystal glass he held. So he knew who the purchasers had been! She was beginning to wish she had not mentioned the matter, when glancing across she saw an ironically amused smile touching his lips. He said:

"I gather that in the new owner of Hollins Hall, the village has acquired not only a famous tycoon, but something of the return of that native." He sounded so disinterested that she felt a stab of relief.

"Yes; it seems that Mr. Fairfax knew both my granddad and my father," she told him. "He appears to be very proud of his Lakeland blood."

"Then that must be counted in his favour." His reply was light, but she was quick to notice that he swiftly turned the subject. "By the way, while I think of it, Dr. McPherson is calling in on me the day after tomorrow, on his way down from Edinburgh to the big conference in London. I know he would be interested to see my notes on that patient who has proved to be rather a success – old Mrs. Pattison. For an advanced case of arthritis she has responded quite splendidly to that new drug I decided to try – which mercifully has not so far shown any adverse side-effects. The case-history makes rather a long report, but if you could manage to do it tomorrow I'd be very grateful. Sorry it's at such short notice, but I only knew Dr. McPherson was coming when I received his letter this morning."

"Of course I'll have it ready," Hilary told him, putting

down her glass and getting up from her chair. "Now I really must be getting home, or my cousin will scold if her cooking spoils. Thank you so much for the drink—" She broke off as opening a drawer he turned towards her, holding out the object he had taken from it. "I think this is yours—"

"My handkerchief! Oh, thanks. I thought I'd lost it and spoilt the set my brother gave me."

"You left it here last night." Somehow his tone was more formal than it had been a few moments ago. As she took the handkerchief their fingers just brushed, and at the contact she felt that sudden odd breathlessness his nearness seemed fated to bring her. She put the square of embroidered linen in her handbag, and glancing up found him smiling down at her, the warmth back in his eyes. If there had been a possible awkward moment it had been successfully bridged – but perhaps it was only her imagination that there had been a touch of constraint in his manner. She said:

"I'm always losing handkerchiefs – it must be a family failing, because Tim is just the same. Cousin Priscilla is constantly scolding about it."

"A surprising failing in such an efficient young woman as yourself!" he observed, seeing her out into the hall. And when having slipped on her coat she went out to where she had left her bicycle against the wall of the house beside the front door: "Watch out at the cross-roads in this twilight – we've had quite enough accident casualties for one week!"

"Yes; and how shocking if I added to them before that report for Dr. McPherson is finished." She laughed over her shoulder at him while she prepared to mount her machine.

"I wasn't thinking of Dr. McPherson. Nevertheless, my desire for your safety was a selfish one," he said coolly. "I'd hate to have to engage a new secretary!"

"I'll take care," she promised. And as she cycled home

in the rapidly gathering darkness, a cold little wind chilling her cheeks, a new warmth penetrated her and she was conscious of rising spirits. It was amazing how rapidly – could that accident only be two days ago? – her relationship with her boss, as Tim always called him, seemed to have developed from a formal, sometimes rather daunting one, to a natural friendliness.

Surely Mrs. Tyson was wrong with her worrying over something that was best left where it belonged – in the dead past? But she still wished the older woman had not confided in her – because it did make for embarrassment when she knew how much he would have hated the knowledge of being discussed.

He had sounded so normal when he mentioned the new arrivals at Hollins Hall – ever rather ironical. It was surely as clear as daylight that however openly Vernon Fairfax might show his dislike for the man his wife had once been engaged to, and however friendly Lena might be prepared to be, Blake regarded the pair of them with no more than bored indifference.

That certainly sent Hilary's spirits, which since Mrs. Tyson's confidences had been unusually low, soaring to quite unexpected heights, and as she approached the long, low lines of Willowbeck Farm with a friendly light giving out a beckoning glow from the window of the kitchen which was Cousin Priscilla's special domain, she hummed a little tune under her breath.

Not that anything she had learned today was really in the least her business! She told herself, opening the gate and bending to pat Shep, who had been patiently awaiting his young mistress's return. Yet somehow it was pleasing to know that whatever Blake and the glamorous Mrs. Fairfax might have once meant to each other, they were now – on his side especially – only the most casual of acquaintances.

Perhaps it was as well for Hilary's peace of mind that

she, along with the rest of humankind, was able to remain unaware of how drastically things were to change in the near future; or of how intricate a web was being woven by those three Grey Sisters who are said to control the destinies of men and women.

CHAPTER SIX

"My treat today, ducky!" Frant announced.

Hilary, mounting the old oak staircase to the restaurant of the Fleece in Kendal, paused, a hand on the banister, to shake a reproving head at her friend.

"Certainly not," she returned firmly. "It's my turn to take you to lunch."

"Then you can consider the dice misthrown and miss your turn!" Frant told her. "I've already told you, a client in New York has sent me an indecently large cheque for her portrait and we're going to celebrate – a miniature hen-party all to ourselves. So don't argue."

"Well, we'll see." Hilary continued up the stairs, and a few moments later the girls were in the pleasant oak-beamed room with its tables of spotless white napery and gleaming silver and glass, which was famous far beyond the bounds of its native Westmorland. It was only half past twelve, but already the majority of the tables were occupied, and a gay hum of conversation rose while customers enjoyed pre-lunch aperitifs.

The girls had driven over from Tarnmere in Frant's rather dashing little open sports car, to spend a pleasant Saturday morning shopping; and now they were more than ready for luncheon. Seeing them, a waitress recognised two favoured habituées, and beamingly bustled them to a corner table.

"It's supposed to have been reserved, but the party is already twenty minutes late, so they can make do with something else, loves!" she announced. "Make yourselves comfy, and I'll come along as soon as I can. But my, what with shortage of staff and folk all squawking to be served at once, you'd best order your drinks now, and I'll see they're sent reet up from the bar!"

"May heaven rain blessings on your head for the angel you are!" Frant told her, and the waitress giggled delightedly. "Two dry Martinis – no, you're *not* going to have a demure sherry," she added as Hilary opened her mouth. "We're cutting a dash (delightful Edwardian expression!) for once in a way. For tuppence I'd order a terribly grand hock – in fact, if we can choose something suitable to go with it, I will!"

"Incurable extravagance!" Hilary tried to sound prim, but her eyes were dancing. "Remember the gentlemen at the tax office!"

"Blights and curses on the gentlemen at the tax office – though I believe they're horribly overworked and have their financial troubles along with the rest of us, poor dears," Frant returned, studying the menu that had been put before her. "I see there's a rather lovely dish of sole and lobster, so hock it shall be; unless you would rather have duck, in which case the sage and onion will insult a Rhine wine, and you shall be regaled on a strong and not too grand Burgundy."

"Sole for me, please," Hilary replied. "Your knowledge of food and wine would completely overawe me if I didn't know you were showing off!"

"How right you are!" her friend grinned at her, and raised her Martini, a glass of which cocktail had been deftly set before each of them. "Here's to us, lovey . . . Lord, how this place is filling up."

"It always does." Hilary sipped her drink, surveying the restaurant, which was growing more crowded every minute, with a feeling of pleasant relaxation.

Frant said suddenly: "Hullo, there are the Vernon Fairfaxes – look, taking that table in the far corner. I don't thing Tarnmere has exactly clasped them to its heart during their month's residence – in spite of the fact that money has splashed about to a quite considerable extent whenever subscriptions have been wanted by the Vicar or various good causes."

"Hardly surprising, considering the dalesfolk value a little courteous interest in their affairs far above money," Hilary commented drily. She glanced across the crowded restaurant to where Lena Fairfax, impeccably groomed in a burgundy ensemble the simplicity of which shrieked *haute couture* to the initiated, her shining hair caught sleekly into the nape of her neck in a style that was at once unfashionable and yet so uniquely her own that it proclaimed the supreme indifference of someone rich enough to ignore contemporary modes. The perfect oval of her face was enhanced by a carefully subdued make-up suitable to the country, and her heavy-shouldered but not unhandsome husband was in grey-blue tweeds with that well-worn look which only a really expensive tailor can create; something a thousand miles away from the slick "newness" of the multiple concerns who cater for the less wealthy majority of the male sex.

Watching them now, Hilary was struck by the look of almost fierce affection he bestowed upon his wife. There was pride there – pride in a lovely, desirable piece of property, but there was more than that. Hilary thought instinctively: *"He's fathoms deep in love with her – far more than she deserves."*

She knew she had glimpsed a fierce, almost devouring passion that was almost frightening in its intensity. A man of strong emotions who, if anything ever happened to arouse his jealousy, could be – dangerous. She wondered how much Lena realised that, if at all. For all the streak of shrewdness beneath that lovely façade she had an idea that there was also a vein of stupidity, born of complete self-satisfaction. And the involuntary thought came to her that it would be as well for young Mrs. Fairfax if she had sufficient sense never to arouse that demon of jealous

87

possessiveness which she – Hilary – felt quite sure lay not far beneath the surface Lena's husband showed the world.

Involuntarily her thoughts went back to that day in John Dallam's shop when she had seen the look of intense dislike Vernon Fairfax had given Blake. Well, he had no need to worry in that direction, thank goodness.

Frant observed, eyeing the newcomers over the rim of her glass: "I just can't really make up my mind. The girl's paintable, but I'm hanged whether I'll consent to do a portrait of her or not." And as Hilary gave her an enquiring glance: "Oh, yes, they didn't take long to find out about me, I'm afraid. I've been first almost commanded, and then, when they found me more than a bit cagey, requested to paint her. I suppose she wants to be hung on the line at next year's Academy. But I'm not at all sure I feel inclined to help!"

"I see." Hilary knew how difficult her friend could be where even quite well known people were concerned if she did not feel like putting them on one of her brilliant canvases. "She would be very ornamental – or so I should have thought."

Frant laughed rather grimly. "That, yes. But as you know, I don't paint for chocolate-boxes, or to my sitters' desires. That one, ducky, is a prize bitch. I should certainly paint what lies behind the mask, and somehow I doubt very much whether she or her devoted spouse would care for the finished product! Though probably he's too infatuated and she too conceited to realise what I'd been about. It takes a very clear-minded person to recognise their inmost self in a ruthless portrait."

"Does it?" As always Hilary was delighted when her friend spoke out about her work, something she could rarely be induced to do.

"Of course it does. As nature had mercifully endowed the plainest women with the best conceit of themselves – instance the elephantine thighs of so many mini-skirt or hot-pants wearers – so that inner veil of self-satisfaction with which all but a very few are endowed draws a veil over a penetrating study of themselves, whether the medium be painting or the written word – though the latter is more easily fathomed, because the most honey-sweet tribute can still imply unpleasant home-truths."

"And you don't think that, however you painted Mrs. Fairfax, she would ever have penetration enough to be offended at your interpretation of her?" Hilary asked.

Frant laughed, her brown eyes suddenly mischievous. "Be worth finding out, maybe," she observed. "Incidentally, they're offering the earth as a fee, which I suppose ought to be an added inducement . . . Why, look who's come in now! No less a person than your boss, and the poor dear obviously isn't going to find an empty table."

She waved, and with a little start Hilary glanced across towards the top of the stairs that led up from street level. Blake was standing, a tall, relaxed figure, brown-haired and very good to look at in that familiar suit of heather tweed, a slight crease between his brows while he glanced round the restaurant. Then, catching sight of Frant's beckoning hand, his face cleared and with a smile he threaded his way through the tables towards them.

"Come and join us, Dr. Kinross," Frant greeted. "If you don't, you'll have to wait a horribly long time for your lunch and everything worth eating will be off the menu."

"That's very kind of you," he answered, pulling out a chair. "If I may share your table—"

"Ah, but I don't mean that at all," Frant told him. "This is a celebration – of an American sale I've made. Do me the honour, dear sir, of being my guest, and you'll give my little party the one touch it needs to be a complete success."

"Indeed! And what, may I ask, is that?" He glanced

89

down at her, his brows raised, the hint of a smile on that rather stern mouth.

"Why, male company that's both ornamental and mentally stimulating, of course!" Frant grinned up at him, and to Hilary's amusement she saw his colour deepen.

"That sounds far too flattering," he observed. "But since you put it so kindly, it would be boorish of me to refuse. So I shall be delighted to be your guest. On the strict understanding that you will allow me to return the compliment –" he glanced at Hilary, that half smile more pronounced, "at an early date. Understood?"

"Entendu!" Frant said briskly, and as he seated himself she waved imperatively for further drinks.

"I'm afraid I can't be too festive," Blake warned. "This is my day off. But I'm driving, and remember the breathalysers! There must be no chance of ruining a medical reputation!"

"It shall be Pepsi-Cola if you wish," his hostess informed him gravely, and while Hilary laughed Blake turned to her, his mouth grave but his own eyes alight. "Miss Frant is making a nonsense of me," he observed. "What is your advice, I wonder?"

"Why, an excellent dry Martini," Hilary told him. "Frant, as you see, is leading me madly astray. So it would be only kind of you to keep me company and so lessen any possible feeling of guilt that may be lurking in the background."

"Then I will, with pleasure," he agreed. "Let's all feel guilty together!"

The gay laughter at their corner table caused Vernon Fairfax to glance across the restaurant, and his heavy brows knitted. Following his glance, his wife gave Frant's little party a long hard stare; then her beautifully made-up lips tightened a moment before she observed with a light laugh:

"Dear me! The local doctor seems very happy. I must

90

confess to being a trifle surprised. I didn't know he could unbend—"

"Who should know better?" her husband asked curtly.

"Don't be silly, Vernon," she replied. "Surely you've forgotten all that nonsense."

He did not answer, but still gazing intently at that opposite corner table, glanced down at her, his hard grey eyes sardonic. "And is there any reason why he shouldn't unbend – now?" he asked. "Those are very ornamental young women. But really, Lena, I should hardly have thought the most avid gossip-monger could have made anything out of a lunch in such a public place as this." He paused, then added drily: *"You* often lunched with him more privately!"

She caught the note of suspicious jealousy, and her laugh was suddenly genuine.

"Darling, why remind me of youthful indiscretions? You must allow me mine, as I have undoubtedly allowed you yours." He reddened, and seeing her advantage she followed it up swiftly. "What one can find attractive in one's salad days can be so infinitely boring a few years later!"

"Not so many years." He was still inclined to be suspicious. "Although you were always as changeable – or should I say volatile, as—"

He paused, and her cascade of laughter sounded musically. "Please don't say as 'the English weather', dear. I refuse to be compared to a television chart!"

"I was going to say, 'as the most changeable of your sex'!" he returned in something of a bulldog attempt to sarcasm.

She laughed again. "Perhaps I was – once upon a time. But not with you, my sweet, not with you."

"Well, see you keep it that way." His hand, strong and sinewy in its possessiveness, suddenly descended on her own as it lay on the snowy white cloth.

91

Again her eyes met his. "Oh, always. Need you doubt it?" she said lightly, and after a moment withdrew her hand. But there had been something in the look he gave her, a flame behind the cold greyness of his eyes that was at once a tribute and a warning. The knowledge that the man she had married could be dangerous as well as possessive filled her with a half triumphant, half scared knowledge; but that was something she would never reveal to him, and as always, she took refuge in half bantering, wholly tantalising withdrawal.

"You must really not treat the world to such a show of fierceness," she observed teasingly. "Otherwise gossip will soon have it that you are too fond of me for us ever to have been married."

It was his turn to raise his brows. "And when have I ever cared for the opinion of others?" he asked with the kind of arrogance that can only come with wealth and power. Then: "Anyway, I'm glad the sight of the fellow hasn't reawakened any – former sentiment. But—"

His stare across the crowded room to where Blake was laughing at something Hilary had said was coldly hostile. That doctor fellow was an arresting-looking chap in his way. Blast him. Even now he hated to think he had once come so near to owning Lena . . .

Smothering a little yawn with one jewelled hand, she begged: "Do let's change this very boring subject, Vernon dear. Let's rather talk about my portrait. Is Frant going to agree to paint me? She's so very sought after, and I must confess to a desire to sit for her."

"She implies that she's booked up," her husband replied gruffly. "I should have thought the fee I mentioned would have changed her mind."

"Darling! Just how stupid can you get! She's a real V.I.P. You can't tempt her that way." Lena sounded genuinely scandalised.

"I don't see why not—" he began, but seeing his scowl-

92

ing gaze on Frant's dark head turned in animated conversation with her guests Lena frowned, laying urgent fingers on her husband's arm.

"For heaven's sake don't let her see you glaring across like that!" she warned. "Or she really will turn me down!"

"Damned impertinence!" Fairfax exclaimed, but he kept the observation muted as the wine list was presented for his consideration.

Quite oblivious as to what was being said at the table on the other side of the room – indeed, she had for the moment forgotten Vernon Fairfax's existence – Hilary was aware of a sense of relaxation and well-being which would have surprised her had she paused to think about it. As it was, she only knew that this little celebration of Frant's had taken on that special glow which she could remember feeling when, as a small girl, something unexpectedly delightful had happened. It had all been enjoyable enough before, but from the moment of Blake's joining them the knowledge that he too, was relaxed and enjoying himself, filled her with a half dreamy contentment. To be so near him, to see his rather stern face light to sudden laughter, to note the quickened interest with which he responded to the various subjects Frant brought up for comment. She was curiously content to relapse into a half dream, listening to her companions' talking; but Frant, her brown eyes going shrewdly from one to the other of her guests, had an unusually thoughtful expression.

After commenting on the bus accident and asking after the mercifully few injured who were still in hospital, Frant observed while an excellent hors d'oeuvres was set before them:

"One thing I have found with those of the medical profession – they're not particularly partial to talking shop: a thing that's supposed to be taboo among many people; and yet, you know, I've seldom met anyone wholly adverse to it. Certainly not among my own kind – artists. It also applies to writers, journalists and above all, the theatrical profession! To each and every one details of their own particular world are of absorbing interest. I sometimes wonder if there are any complete exceptions."

"Property developers, perhaps," Hilary suggested. "One could hardly imagine them eagerly beguiling leisure moments with swopping comments on their latest concrete monstrosities, or how lovely it must be to demolish another Georgian square, or lay waste yet one more charming village. But maybe I'm wrong."

With the arrival of the main course Frant's extremely extravagant choice of a remarkably fine hock made its appearance. Dr. Kinross's brows shot up at the sight of the label, and went still higher when he savoured the pale golden wine's exquisite bouquet and flavour.

"I am doubly honoured," he observed. "Frant, your choice is entitled to win an overwhelming accolade from the most exacting club in St. James's – and I'm only able to tell you that by having been taken to such places by my extreme seniors! Where, may I ask, were you so well educated?"

Frant's cheeks were tinged with pleasure as she raised her own glass. "My father," she explained. "He was no wine snob, bless him, but he *did* know what was what. Anyway, what he taught me has won me respect in various countries."

"I only know it tastes like the nearest thing to nectar this side of Olympus," Hilary agreed. "Here's to the sale in New York, Frant darling – and I only hope your buyer appreciates your picture as she ought to do!"

The rest of the meal passed off very pleasantly, and as they lingered over their coffee the restaurant gradually began to empty. Then, while they were deep in conversation a sudden shadow fell across their table, and a familiar light brittle voice said:

"I really can't go without a word of greeting. How are you, Miss Frant – and you, Blake? For once not too busy to be social . . . No, please don't get up!"

"And how is little Hilary Talgarth? Nice to see you here." This time it was Vernon Fairfax who spoke with somewhat pointed emphasis, smiling with genuine warmth at Hilary.

"Oh, Miss Talgarth! How are you? I didn't realise you were here," said Lena, and turning to Frant again, "What a charming place this is – so delightful to find somewhere that gives one really good English food instead of execrable flambée affairs! If only English restaurant owners would abstain from would-be elaborate continental things that may be excellently done at the Vefours or the Paris Ritz, but are quite disastrously out of place in the countryside here, don't you agree?"

"Oh, indeed," Frant assured with a cool poise that somehow made the other girl's observations seem exactly what they were – a trifle over-elaborate and off-key. Lena, for all her worldly sophistication, yet had a slightly unfortunate habit of over-airing the knowledge her travels with a rich husband had brought her. Glancing at Vernon Fairfax, Hilary was aware of the displeasure his wife's bad manners had caused, while he continued to talk to her, and in his turn ignore the others.

"*Do* sit down, Blake," Lena requested again. "You're so tall you loom quite alarmingly under these delightful oak beams! Are you two—" her smile became a little fixed as she looked round at Hilary, "taking a day off from the round of medical duties? I feel sure you must more than earn it."

"Miss Frant has been kindly and magnificently lunching me," said Blake. "We were discussing the excellent cellar here. I find my hostess is not only an artist in her own line of country."

Frant laughed. " 'Good wine needs no bush'. And to

my mind together with good food is part of civilisation. Aren't I right, Mr. Fairfax?"

For once the tycoon looked slightly startled. "Why, yes – indeed you're right," he agreed, and then with a smile warmer than Hilary had yet seen in him. "So you are not, I take it, one of those orange juice and toast young artists?"

"Definitely not," Frant returned. "My father was a connoisseur. His knowledge of port was encyclopaedic, but I'm afraid I detest it! But as I like to reserve my own knowledge for celebratory purposes, and stick to soft drinks while I'm working, I don't often get a chance to air my own fairly limited knowledge of good wine!"

"And you do keep so marvellously slender!" exclaimed Lena. "Well, we must be on our way. Do come and sample *our* cellar soon. They must, mustn't they, Vernon?"

"Of course. We'll hope to be seeing you." Fairfax, motioning his wife to follow, walked towards the top of the stairs. Lena had reached it when she stopped and turned back. Beside Frant's table again she said:

"I *must* ask! Have you given any more thought to little me? Do you think it will be possible, while we're up here, that you might find time to fit me in? I know you must be packed up with commissions, and it's really an imposition to keep on bothering you, but it *would* be so wonderful of you—"

There was a brief silence while Frant considered the slender elegance of the figure before her with a clear, hard stare that made Hilary want to laugh, and indeed cost her an effort to keep her face straight. It must be so very seldom that the rich Mrs. Fairfax had to plead for something she so obviously wanted very badly indeed. Then:

"I think it rather probable that something can be done," Frant said. "May I telephone you tomorrow?"

"Oh, do! I'll be in all day." Lena's smile became dazzling. "And if I catch a cold or go off colour, Blake here will

96

be on hand to give medical aid! 'Bye now!" And with an airy wave she followed her husband down the stairs.

There was a short silence in which Blake selected a cigar, and carefully cut and lit it. It was Hilary who spoke first, her eyes mischievous.

"So you've decided to paint the lady!" she observed. "I somehow thought you would."

"Well, she's very paintable – and I think I can do something presentable," Frant's tone was caustic. "But I'm not very partial to empty shells, however beautiful they may appear on the surface." She looked at Blake. "Do I sound bitchy? But I paint the truth, not what people want to see. Yet, as I was telling Hilary the other day, it's amazing how seldom either the sitter or the sitter's relations tumble to what I've been up to!"

"I know just what you mean," he agreed. "Look at those Sargents in the Tate – especially that one of the self-made Edwardian financier! I doubt if any of those eminent people realised how the artist stripped them of all pretensions, and left their weaknesses and vanity for posterity to smile over."

"Sargent – lord, lord, how very flattering you're being!" Frant laughed, a flush of pleasure tinging her cheeks. "But believe me, it makes a pleasant change when one can paint a subject who has something really lovely, with an inward charm that can cast a glow."

"Yes, it must be." Blake's tone was a little absent, while his eyes went unconsciously to Hilary's profile – noting the charming way her red-gold hair grew above her creamy forehead, the sweetness yet strength of her lips, the charming way her nose tilted very slightly, the roundness of a chin that hinted at strength of character . . .

Watching her guests, it was Frant's turn to give a mischievous little smile. She said casually:

"You wouldn't believe the number of times I've tried to get this lass to sit for me, and – would you believe it! – I've

97

never succeeded in doing so. But I shall one day, and then there'll be a portrait worth painting – and worth possessing too!"

Hilary started, and looked round quickly, the colour flowing up delicately under her skin. "You're talking nonsense," she said. "You don't want to waste your time on me, as I've often told you."

"That's for me to decide – finally," her friend returned, and with a sidelong glance at Blake: "Don't you agree?"

"Indeed I do!" he answered succinctly. But there was no doubting the sudden warmth in his eyes as, glancing up, Hilary's embarrassed gaze fleetingly met his own. "Certainly you must make her sit for you," he said firmly. "It would be sheer folly not to."

"Ah, an ally!" Frant observed triumphantly. "I shall continue to bully until I get my way."

But neither of her companions were fully attending to her. Her earlier words were echoing in Blake's ears as he watched Hilary's confusion – her downcast eyes contemplating her coffee cup with apparent rapt attention.

"A portrait worth painting – and worth possessing too!"

And it came to him in a sudden blinding flash that those words did not only apply to a portrait as yet unpainted – they applied with far greater strength to the glowing charm and loveliness of the original. A girl who, his heart and mind were both suddenly telling him, would indeed be worth possessing. . . .

While Hilary, her heart fluttering like the wings of a caged bird in her breast, still refused to meet the intent blue-grey stare which she knew was upon her. But though she dared not look up, she was aware in every fibre of her being of his nearness, of the quiet strength of him; knew, too, that from this hour so casually begun in Frant's "little celebration" there could be no turning back. Her heart was no longer her own, and never would be again.

CHAPTER SEVEN

WITH an impatient gesture Lena Fairfax stubbed out her fourth Turkish cigarette in the hour, and pushed the white jade ash-tray impatiently away from her, careless of the hot sparks that fell on the faded walnut of the exquisite Queen Anne table that stood beside the winged chair upholstered in mulberry-coloured and gold brocade in which she was reclining.

With a swift movement of lithe, almost cat-like grace she rose, and crossing the deep-piled Chinese carpet of pale rose and turquoise, a colour scheme echoed in the fabulous hand-made wallpaper with which the walls of the long, beautifully proportioned sitting-room were hung, she walked to the deep recess where french windows draped with turquoise velvet framed a breathtaking view of the lake and valley of Tarnmere spread in a panorama of green and blue, environed by its ring of distant, still snow-capped mountains.

The fact that this setting was really far too exotic for any country house did not even occur to the girl who stood looking out at the almost breathtakingly lovely view, a discontented droop to her wilful mouth. She had started out by deciding to – in her own words – "Go madly super-rustic", which meant that she had decided to furnish the whole of the big, rambling old house, which was partly Elizabethan, with Jacobean additions, in Tudor oak to match the honey-coloured panelled walls of the dining-room.

There, elaborately carved seventeenth-century chairs in faded tapestry of olive green and dull claret stood round the walls, facing a great oval table of satin-sheened golden oak. A board around which had once echoed the mirth and revelry of periwigged, high-booted cavaliers in silks and laces; of ladies whose gracefully curling ringlets fell tantalisingly on to the loveliness of ivory-white shoulders rising from gowns of rich brocades and silks. How many languishing glances, soulful sighs, or shy, deeper avowals of love had been whispered; too often to be severed for ever by the bitter unhappiness of Civil War and valiant death in the cause of that Charles whose last wintry months had ended on the scaffold in Whitehall; or perhaps to have a happy ending many years later when his gay and ever-romantic son "came to his own again", had been witnessed by those mellow walls. None of which whispers from the romantic past could ever have possessed the least interest for their present owner.

But after motoring many miles and ransacking numerous antique shops far grander than that of John Dallam, Lena had soon tired of what she now pronounced "too gloomily North of England, Vernon darling", and had reverted to the usual luxury which she deemed an essential background for her wherever she made what she was pleased to call a home.

For the first weeks of this Lakeland spring the old house on its wooded ledge amid skilfully landscaped gardens far above the emerald-turfed bordered oval of pale aquamarine which was Tarnmere Lake, had delighted and refreshed her jaded mind. But now the novelty had worn off long ago; and though there had been a visit to London, a trip across to Paris for the Spring Collections, and a week in Monte Carlo, she knew she was beginning to more than regret this latest and perhaps oddest whim of her husband's.

The fact that he was often away, and yet seemed when he returned from his numerous business trips to be more relaxed and human than she had ever known him, going off with local climbers on old and familiar hill climbs, counted for little with Lena, who was as always far too wrapped up in her own selfish desires to take note of either the wishes or feelings of anyone else: perhaps least of all those of the man she had married.

All that really mattered now was that she was bored. Bored as she had so often been, but with a new and deeper sense of frustration which was beginning to chafe her to a growing irritation – with herself, with Vernon; in fact with everyone and everything surrounding her in the cocoon of opulent yet shallow luxury which she deemed essential to her selfish existence.

There was something else even more important which she was missing. Male admiration. Something in which it was the breath of life for her to bask. Up here there was no lack of it, of course – from elderly gentlemen whose wives were apt to eye her with thinly veiled dislike; from young men who, to her sophisticated mind, were often good-looking enough, but either shy and tongue-tied before glamour they had not previously encountered, or else were wrapped up in affairs of farm and estate of which they were all too often fatally ready to impart the most boring of details. Conversations to which she was forced to listen with a fixed smile, a falsely polite air of intense interest, and a mounting desire to scream!

It did nothing to lessen her irritation to know that Vernon, though a sardonic observer of her increasing boredom, possessed a potential jealousy, though he had always been the indulgent elder husband, ready to view his wife's numerous admirers with faintly amused contempt. But she was only too well aware that he had never been anything but supremely assured of both himself and her; a sureness which was born of the money and power that ruled all things in his life.

Yet Lena knew – and resented the knowledge – that once his jealousy was really roused, she would be pulled up with the ruthless crack of the whip that so far remained invisible. Though her own arrogance and conceit had covered this knowledge with the belief that it was "really not difficult to twist Vernon round one's little finger".

Since coming to Tarnmere she had received two shocks. The first was the fact that for once, knowing she was "bored stiff", her husband was not prepared immediately to uproot himself and move on to "fresh woods and pastures new". His return to the dales where he had been born seemed to have roused a determination to stay, anyway for some time, in this newest house of his. When she complained of ennui, he had for once showed a quiet obstinacy which she found rather daunting. He had been ready enough to acquiesce in her trips to London, Paris and Monte Carlo, even to agree that she should spend a week in Rome quite soon. But he had told her:

"I've not been back here since I was a youth, and although I'll have to be away quite a lot, I have a desire to see spring and summer, and maybe early autumn up here." And when she had hunched an impatient shoulder, he reminded her: "It isn't often I ask you to consider my wishes, but this time I mean you to."

And wise for once, she had agreed, and tried to find comfort from filling the house with a series of week-end guests, whose noisy and brash behaviour generally earned the disapproval of not only the villagers, but the owners of the other big houses, who would normally have cultivated the new owners of Hollins Hall. But as she felt "the county" was just too boring and dowdy, Lena shrugged that aside. But the distance from London to Lakeland weather soon made her smart friends find excuses not to come, and by now she was feeling very cut off from the people who "spoke one's own language", as she put it.

She told her husband with some acidity: "Of course stay here if you wish. I suppose when I want some excitement I can always go out and snip off the faded roses! Perhaps you would also like me to learn to milk the cows? I understand you own a herd of the most ornamental Jerseys?"

"No, my dear. I'm quite aware that you regard this as no Petit Trianon, and I doubt if ever Marie Antoinette carried her dairymaiding to such lengths," he answered with that unexpected sarcasm which somehow always had the power to disconcert her. "You may remember that there was another bored and restless lady who would have been far wiser to settle down and control her passion for self-indulgence!"

She regarded him sulkily, then gave one of her high, rather hard laughs. "Are you suggesting there's any danger of *my* losing my head? Is that why you're parking me up here? Couldn't you by now have learned to trust me without including rustication in your plans for me?"

"Nothing could have been further from my thoughts," he returned imperturbably.

She gave him a considering look. "Was that meant to be a compliment, or the opposite?" And as he only smiled: "Oh, very well, have your own way. But it would serve you right if you suddenly found I'd run off with a handsome farmer!"

His smile broadened, and a sudden little spurt of resentment made her go further than she had intended to. "Or what about the local doctor? He's grown into a bit of a dull stick now he's older, but I'm sure many of his female patients must consider him far from unattractive!"

She had the satisfaction, from the way the smile had been instantly wiped off his face, of knowing that she had succeeded in flicking him on the raw. Yet the moment the words were out she wished the jibe unspoken.

There was a moment's silence. Then his next words fell like ice into the silence.

"You've just assured me you were in no danger of losing your head, Lena. I trust that you'll never be fool enough to – prove me wrong."

The iron note in his voice frightened her, but she met the sudden hard stare of those cold grey eyes, with a laugh, a shrug, and a drawled: "It's you who are being the fool now, Vernon darling. Do let's stop nattering about foolish things, and sit down and enjoy a drink together. Tell me how you got on in New York—"

But the remembrance of that flare of jealousy had given her pause for thought at the time, and had remained at the back of her mind ever since. And now she was remembering it again while she moved restlessly back into the room, her own face hard and unsmiling while she lit another cigarette.

Confound Vernon and his suspicions! Today, like everyone and everything, he was no more than a bore – a barrier to making life the fun it ought to be!

There was one person here who could make life – more interesting. Being of the type who wants to eat her cake and have it, she knew she was wanting to see more of Blake Kinross. Somehow she could not believe that the man who had been so deeply in love with her had entirely lost all interest. Anyway, it would be interesting to find out. Besides, his persistent refusal to renew their acquaintance intrigued her. Of course, he was the local doctor and if she was ill he would have to attend to her. Unfortunately she was remarkably healthy, and she knew it would be no use pretending otherwise. Blake would know at once if she was putting on an act—

She was thinking now, with a sense of intense pique, that he had not so much avoided as ignored her. At least – and here her vanity and pride came to aid her annoyance – that was being rather foolish. No fate, kindly or otherwise, had thrown them in each other's way, since she had been perfectly healthy and in no need of any medical advice! So it was natural that their paths should not have crossed, apart from an occasional encounter in the village, a passing of cars on the road with a careless wave from herself, and a distantly polite acknowledgement from the doctor.

Yet now, as so often during these last few weeks, an unwelcome memory returned to strengthen her resentment. The memory of that day in the restaurant at Kendal when he had been lunching with those two girls – one of whom had been his secretary, and with whom he had so very obviously been on the most cordial of terms! It would not have mattered if the girl had been plain or unnoticeable; but she was not. Hilary Talgarth might be quiet and unobtrusive, but with that red-gold hair, those undoubted good looks and a poise which had the power to irritate the so much more glamorous Mrs. Vernon Fairfax, that interval at the Fleece still had the power to annoy.

And yet why should it? What a *fool* I'm being! she told herself for perhaps the twentieth time as she paced the room, the curling smoke from her cigarette narrowing her eyes against the recollection. Whoever Blake Kinross chose to be friendly with should be a matter only of the most supreme indifference to her. Or ought to have been.

Ought to have been! With Hamlet she might have uttered the bitter comment: "Ay, there's the rub!" For Blake's preferences did not, could not leave her in the rôle of sardonic onlooker. There was still something in those tawny good looks, that cool poise which he had developed since the days when she had had him at her feet, which had the power to disturb her far more than she would admit, even in those moments when she was most frank with herself. It angered her always self-inflated self-esteem to think he might even contemplate putting another girl in the place she had left vacant.

However, there was one satisfactory result of that annoying day: Veronica Frant had finally consented to do a portrait in oils of Mrs. Vernon Fairfax; which was not only a social triumph to be casually alluded to, thereby arousing jealous fury in the breasts of one's dearest friends in all the smartest places, but a compliment to one's own looks! The picture was still in its early stages, locked up for the most part in a room set apart as a studio for Frant, whose visits aroused a genuine enthusiasm in the sitter, which she was far from guessing the artist did not in the least reciprocate.

("Nothing so low as the artist's humble studio for the great Mrs. V. F., ducky," had been Frant's caustic comment to Hilary. "She must be 'at ease in her own surroundings, so much better, don't you think?' Well, *I* couldn't care less, and to be treated as a V.I.P. at Hollins Hall I find amusing, if faintly nauseating. I trust she'll be conceited enough to find the finished product flattering.")

Lena was so pleased to have at last obtained the artist's consent that she had not even protested at Frant's insisting she should have the key of the room in which the painting stood, in her own possession. Frant had said charmingly, but with a hint of iron:

"While I'm on a portrait, no one – I repeat, *no one* – must look at it. Until we're finished, that must be my stipulation. I do hope you won't mind, Mrs. Fairfax?"

And recognising that for once she had met a will stronger than her own, Lena had replied quite meekly:

"Of course. If you feel that way I'm more than ready to agree."

"So sweet of you," Frant told her affably. "No doubt I'm being most trying, but you must bear with an artist's whims, Mrs. Fairfax."

("Which means," Frant observed to Hilary, "that I shall not be bothered with Mrs. F.'s dearest friends crowding in to see the half-finished portrait with such comments as 'Don't you think the mouth a trifle too hard, darling? . . . The eyes a little too remote?' I'm painting her not only because she wants me to, but because I find her interesting. But I'm hanged if I'll put up with any 'friendly criticisms' meantime. Any of that nonsense, and they could use the darned canvas on a fifth of November bonfire!")

Hilary had regarded her friend gravely. "Frant," she observed, "I love you very much, but I'm of the opinion that you can be a callous bitch!"

The eminent artist opened wide amber eyes at her. "Hilary love," she returned, "like all quiet observers you have the most disconcerting way of arriving at the exact truth!" At which they had both dissolved in laughter.

Of these exchanges young Mrs. Fairfax naturally had no knowledge. Her ego continued to be inflated by the realisation that she was to be immortalised as "a Frant portrait", in all probability to be hung on the line at Burlington House, and that knowledge was more than enough to make her almost purr.

Wrapped in such sublime egotism, she could not have had less interest in what Tarnmere village itself thought of her. At first prepared to take the new lady of Hollins Hall on slightly suspicious approval, a few weeks of Lena's presence among them had changed incipient good-will if not to hostility, to slightly scornful indulgence of an "off-come" who had failed to make the grade – an opinion which was pungently stated by Mr. Hardisty whose ver-dict, delivered over the grocery counter, was not without weight.

"Ah," he observed darkly, "when *I* was a lad there were ladies at the big houses whom one could reckon with! But this Mrs. Fairfax, for all her grand and mighty ways, isn't one of that sort at all! As for Vernon Fairfax – weren't his folk, when all's said and done, farming folk in a small way, with a cousin who kept a beer-house up on t'Raise? Good enough bodies as the rest of us, but nowt so grand as give this young madam her airs and graces! Not one that Tarnmere'll ever take to, or she to us, for her mind's off and away to grander places, which is no doubt right in such a lass who it's plain to see lives only for pleasuring.

Here today and gone tomorrow, that's the way it'll be. Mark my words and see if I'm not reet!"

And the village, which was accustomed to smile at the old gentleman and laugh indulgently at his memories of bygone days, in this case was inclined to listen, take note, nod knowing heads and wag ready tongues.

None of which could have mattered less to Mrs. Fairfax while she restlessly paced the colourful luxury of her sitting-room, trying to think up a defence against boredom.

Then suddenly her fingers, which had been absently tapping one of the panes in the long window at which she paused, ceased their movement.

A party! That must be the answer. A party, which if it must include a good many fairly ghastly people, would yet break the stifling monotony, and at least cause a deal of talk and admiration in the neighbourhood.

Once the idea had taken root it began to fill her with a growing pleasurable anticipation. The occasion should be something really exciting: a champagne cocktail party of which the district would talk for weeks. However little she might care for what the villagers thought of her, she cared greatly for the impact that the new hostess at Hollins Hall should make on the local County families. People such as old Lady Davenham at Yewdale Manor, and Major-General Sir Arthur Blakeney and his somewhat formidable spouse, who lived across the lake. And of course those rather terrifying spinster sisters, the Misses Aurelia and Maria Skelwith, last of a family of quite awe-inspiring antiquity – whose thirteenth-century tombs in the little church bore effigies unnervingly like the last two of their line!

And then of course there must be a fair sprinkling of others, many of whom like the Talgarths at Willowbeck Farm had known Vernon's people in the past before his entire family had left the district. At the thought of the

Talgarths she frowned, but Vernon would want them invited; and of course their family *had* lived in the same house since the time of Elizabeth Tudor . . . And Blake Kinross must certainly be one of the guests, even if she had to drag him here, whether Vernon liked it or not. And even Vernon couldn't object to Blake being under his roof at the same time as two or three score other guests.

As usual, when an idea took hold of her Lena was at once impatient to put a plan of campaign into action. A date must be decided upon, invitations sent – a list should be drawn up tomorrow. And then of course the details of the catering arranged. Champagne, laced with brandy and bitters, should flow like water, with fruit-cups for any who might dislike or be unable to cope with the more potent offering. A substantial buffet, including delicacies of smoked salmon and caviar, would make the occasion a very different affair from those dreary cocktail parties at which one never got anything to eat except horrible little canapés with no particular taste, *petites saucisses* on sticks, or those unspeakable "dips" which had far too little substance to enable guests to carry their drinks. On this occasion the food should be as lavish as the drink, and the party would be talked of for long afterwards! Even if the County disapproved, curiosity would bring them.

Her discontented expression replaced by a little smile of anticipation, she was about to turn away from the window when she caught sight of a car on the road that wound below the terraced garden. It had evidently broken down or was in trouble of some kind, for a man was bending over the open engine.

She glanced down casually, and then suddenly her whole body tensed and she leaned forward, her gaze intent. For some moments she watched the man tinkering with the engine, then turning from the window she crossed the room swiftly, and opening the door, a moment or so later was running lightly up the stairs and along the corridor leading off the minstrels' gallery to her own room. There her housecoat was discarded for a tweed suit which she donned at six times her usual pace of dressing; and while she buttoned the elegant smoke-grey jacket, looked down from the window which gave the same view as the one from the sitting-room. The car was still there, and its owner could be seen, even at this distance, to be standing by it in obvious exasperation.

So something really was wrong! A smile of satisfaction touched her lips. Surveying her reflection in the long mirror of the white-and-gold fitted wardrobe, she made one or two skilful touches to her already almost perfect make-up, and then ran downstairs again.

Five minutes later, having descended the winding garden paths to the front gate of wrought-iron between two pillars of the same grey stone that lined the road to the lake, she went through them and called gaily to the man who stood regarding his car, a frown of deep annoyance on his good-looking countenance.

"Blake! What's wrong? Your car seems to have chosen to let you down at our very gates!"

Blake turned with a visible start as his name was spoken. Then: "So it appears," he said. "Good afternoon."

"Any idea what's wrong?" she asked, ignoring the formality of his greeting.

"Your guess is as good as mine. The whole darned thing has failed – even the lights won't work. She was going as smoothly as usual, when suddenly she just went dead on me."

"How lucky it isn't pouring with rain for once in a way," Lena observed sympathetically. "You must let Charles, our chauffeur, take a look – I've often told Vernon that he's much too much of a Cockney rough diamond for a Rolls, but he's an absolute wizard with every sort of engine. If it's a really big job you can come in and telephone the garage—" She turned towards the gate again.

"No, really – please don't bother. I can easily walk to the village and tell them to fetch the wretched machine. Luckily, I'm not on my rounds, or an urgent case," he told her.

"Don't be so silly," Lena called over her shoulder. "With an expert on the premises – Why, there he is talking to the gardener." She beckoned imperatively, and the chauffeur came quickly in response to her: "Charles! I want you at once!"

Charles, very tall and smart in chauffeur's claret-coloured uniform, with a sharp Cockney's face, whom Blake recognised from that night of the bus accident, came down the terraced paths at the double.

"Yes, madam?" He arrived with a quick salute.

"Dr. Kinross's car has gone back on him. Would you see just how bad the trouble is? Or maybe you can get things started again easily."

"Very good, madam." Charles saluted Blake, who smiled ruefully at him, saying:

"I'll be much obliged if you can get her going again. Whatever's wrong is quite beyond my not particularly extensive engineering knowledge."

"In fact, you know far more about human insides than machines," Lena observed with a laugh.

"You never spoke a truer word." She noted with secret satisfaction that, though his eyes were on the chauffeur and not herself, he had sounded warmer and more natural than he had done since their first meeting at John Dallam's.

After a few minutes' expert scrutiny the chauffeur looked up and shook his head. "I'm afraid your magneto's had it, sir," he informed Blake. "It's a case for the garage all right."

Repressing the extrmely pungent word of masculine exasperation ready to spring to his lips, Blake said calmly:

"Thanks very much. I'll telephone Garsides to send along their breakdown van."

"I'll do that for you, sir," Charles offered. He had seen the expression in the doctor's eyes, noted the tightening of his mouth and, as he expressed himself later to his cronies at the White Lion: "Lor', if ever I see a gent wanting to let himself go and not being able to because of me lady forcing him to button his lip, that was the doc! But he *is* a gent, and that's a fact—"

"Aye, and so he is, and we don't need thee telling us so!" observed a local in whom rather too much strong beer had inflamed to a pitch of quite unnecessary patriotism. "Let any say otherwise, and he can coom outside and prove who's reet with a round or two—"

But this was met with general disapproval and a – "Learn to hold thy beer, Tom!" While Charles only laughed and stood another, quite different sort of round.

Now as Blake passed him a note exchanged hands, and the doctor told him: "Ask them to be as quick as they can, will you? Somehow the car must be got into working order by tomorrow morning. I've a busy day ahead."

"Don't you worry, sir!" Charles threw another crashing salute, and with some reluctance Blake followed his hostess up to the house. She took him into the library, first issuing an imperative order to the butler.

"You look tired, Blake, I've ordered tea, but if you'd rather have it I'll call for whisky and soda."

"Tea sounds delightful. But you're being much too kind," he said.

"But no, the kindness is all on your side, I assure you." She leaned back, her eyes smiling across at him with the sort of intimacy he was far from appreciating. "Vernon is away for a few days, on one of his interminable business trips, and I'm bored, bored, bored. So don't blame me for welcoming this – most blameless interlude. And for heaven's sake do stop sounding so formal!" Her cascade of laughter was undoubtedly attractive. "There are servants galore around, you know, so there's not the slightest danger to your reputation, medical or otherwise!"

"I never imagined there was," he returned coolly, leaning forward to flick a lighter to the cigarette she had just selected. "No, I won't smoke, thank you."

"Oh!" She opened her eyes wide at him – a trick that he had once found captivating, but no longer had the least power to fascinate him: "Are you one of those frightening doctors who threaten the smoker of the odd cigarette with a dire and dreadful death?"

"Not at all. The occasional cigarette can be perfectly harmless, but," his eyes went to the filled ashtray on the table beside her chair, "I would – if I were your medical adviser – warn you that it would be wise to cut down quite considerably."

"But of course you'll be my medical adviser." She smiled at him through a spiral of blue smoke. "There's no one else in Tarnmere, is there? But as I haven't yet called you in officially this visit may be invested with the utmost propriety – and I'll *still* promise to try to smoke less if you tell me to."

With inward irritation he realised that he was being put in a somewhat vulnerable position. But his face remained a polite mask while he observed: "I only smoke a pipe, which would be quite out of place here."

"How madly male and healthy of you!" It was hard to tell whether her light tone was slightly mocking or not. "Vernon sticks to his eternal cigars – and heaven knows, they cling to the curtains enough, but I suppose I've got used to it." She sat up, stubbing out her cigarette as the butler appeared in stately splendour bearing a heavy silver tray on which reposed a delicate Staffordshire tea service nearly two hundred years old. The assortment of sandwiches accompanying the fragrant China tea with thin slices of lemon was exquisitely chosen, as were the small cakes that followed. It was only when she was filling his cup for the second time that Lena asked abruptly:

"Do you really enjoy being a doctor up here – so far away from any real civilisation?"

"Certainly I do; otherwise I shouldn't be doing it. As for 'real civilization', that's a term which very much depends on one's personal definition," he said drily.

"Well, I would rather call Harley Street and its environs the centre of medical civilisation – and learning." She gave him a direct look. "I haven't forgotten what Sir Keith Lowson said about you years ago. He was quite certain you were going to the top; and you must know yourself how highly he thought of your prospects when you were at St. Winifred's. Strangely enough," she added, picking up her cup and saucer, "I met him at a party not long ago – one of those charity affairs at the Savoy. He mentioned you and wondered where you'd got to." She laughed. "When I said I was of the opinion that you were stupidly wasting yourself somewhere in the North, he answered, 'Oh, I wouldn't say that, my dear. He'll be doing what he wants among people whom he cares for. All the best doctors don't dwell between Wigmore Street and Regent's Park, you know!' I really felt quite snubbed."

It was Blake's turn to laugh and a faint tinge of colour was in his tanned cheeks. "That sounds just like the old boy, bless him. I should never have been really happy in London." He leaned back in his chair, and there was a touch of sardonic in the smile he gave her. "You chose very wisely, Lena. We should soon have found how very ill-suited we were, and how different our idea about almost everything under the sun would have been."

"That's obvious – now," she agreed. "And yet when I married Vernon, did it leave you so completely indifferent? I thought at the time you were – rather fond of me."

There was a moment's silence. She watched him closely, but there was nothing to be read in the sudden sphinx-like mask his face had become. His next words startled her.

"When you threw me over," he said deliberately, "I went through hell. But no experience is without its value, however unlikely that may seem at the time. And now you have the life you chose, with all its attendant pleasures, and an obviously devoted husband. I have my career and a life which, little though you may credit it, is of infinite pleasure to me. So let the past bury the past and lie forgotten. Don't you agree?"

He spoke with an indifference that somehow had the power both to irritate and sting her pride. Not to admit to one scar! But her tone was light as she responded:

"I couldn't agree more. And just to show that the present is quite untouched by the past, I do hope you'll come to a party I'm giving here in a fortnight's time. Nothing formal – just champagne cocktails and a buffet. You'll meet a lot of your local chums, and it will be all great fun. Now don't say you'll be too busy, because people are bound to be disappointed if you don't appear. Vernon will be home, and it will be something in the nature of a housewarming. I haven't given a formal one yet."

His hesitation was perceptible but only momentary. After all, it would be rather boorish to refuse. He said:

"Thank you. I'll certainly be glad to come so long as no emergency crops up. Doctors are always the most unreliable prospective guests, I'm afraid."

"Then you shall be sent a card. And you'll promise not to make up some excuse at the last moment?" Her smile was warm; she was aware of an odd triumph in having obtained his acceptance with such comparative ease. She had a shrewd idea that if his car had not broken down at the very gate of Hollins Hall he would have written a polite refusal. As it was—

"Certainly I shan't. I have many faults, but I always do

my best to keep a promise." He glanced at his wrist-watch. "I'm afraid surgery hours loom and I must be walking back, leaving my wretched car to wait for the garage people to tow her ignominiously through the village."

"Certainly you're not walking back. Charles has his orders, and the Rolls will be waiting to run you home," she told him, rising as he did and holding out her hand as in response to a touch on the bell beside her the butler appeared in the doorway. "Goodbye—or rather, *au revoir*, Doctor." Her eyes were teasing while he took her hand, his bow a little formal. "We shall meet on the night of my party."

"Emergencies apart, most certainly. Thank you again, both for my tea and your chauffeur's help."

Then he was gone, and a few minutes later watching his tall figure get into the Rolls she saw him glance up, and waved. He waved back, then the big car glided out on to the winding road and out of sight; but still she stood where she was, biting the tip of one slim finger thoughtfully.

What a—very welcome as well as unexpected interlude; and what an acquisition for the party the date of which she would now decide! All bordeom vanished, she moved across to the Queen Anne walnut bureau and seating herself at it, consulted a desk calendar before drawing a sheet of expensive writing paper towards her.

But, pen in hand, she did not immediately make any notes. She glanced across to the winged chair in which Blake had so lately been seated.

Seeing him there in her own setting for the first time, it occurred to her that his handsomeness, that hint of virile toughness behind his quiet manner, had supplied the one detail which was wanted to make life all it should be. Her admirers, casual or foreign and ardent, had never had the same power of rousing that feeling in her. And suddenly she felt it was inevitable that, seeing him in the same chair

116

where Vernon so often sat, she should compare him to that other whom she had married – not to Vernon Fairfax's advantage. Vernon was good-looking enough in his way, of course, one could even call him distinguished; but his hair was greying at the temples, the lines of a life of constant work and the strain of high finance were deeply etched on his face; and with his big shoulders, thickened neck, and mouth that held that hint of the ruthless power which even when he was most tender and indulgent towards her, she sometimes found him a little repellent.

That such a thought was the basest ingratitude never occurred to her shallow heart or mind. She only knew that, now she had met Blake Kinross again, even while she faintly resented his apparent complete indifference over that broken engagement, this afternoon had brought a new excitement into her life.

Vernon would not like Blake coming to the party at all! But he would just have to put up with it. A little smile touched her mouth as she put pen to paper, choosing a date two weeks away. After all, there would be plenty of guests, it was not as if this were to be an intimate dinner party for just a few; anyone who *was* anyone for miles around, and a good many who were nobodies in particular, would be present, and even Vernon with his stupid dislike of Blake couldn't make a fuss about the local doctor being invited. Regarding this afternoon's little interlude – well, Vernon need never be told about that. As for inviting Blake to a more intimate party – hum! her smile widened slightly. That might come later!

CHAPTER EIGHT

"That's the lot for this afternoon, Hilary. I've got to rush off now – young Mrs. Dalston's baby seems to have decided to condescend to come into the world some days late, so I'll sign the letters on my return. Of course Dalston is in the usual father-to-be near-hysterics, but obviously hoping it will be a son and heir to carry on that particular farming line! Talk about the stronger sex – in my line of business they positively sometimes fill me with shame!"

"Don't I know it! The fuss there's been in a ward over some heavyweight wailing he 'can't swallow such big pills, Nurse!'" Hilary laughed. "I'll soon have these letters finished – is there anything else you want doing?"

"Only for you to take yourself off as soon as you're through and get out into the sunshine."

"Thank you. I will," she replied, and returned his hasty gesture of farewell as he closed the office door and went out to his car at a half run, having snatched up his case from the hall stand where it always stood ready.

As she listened to the sound of the car's engine dying away in the distance, Hilary's hands, busy on the typewriter keyboard, were suddenly stilled. She stared out of the window with unseeing eyes. Would it always be like this? To have one's heart (so stupidly no longer one's own, now or for ever again) seem to turn right over at the sight of a tall figure, a lean, handsome face, a man's deep attractive tones. To have to be near someone, working with that same someone, day after day, loving and not daring to show that love.

Worst of all perhaps were those moments when it was fatally easy to imagine a sudden warmth in that sherry-coloured glance holding her own, an added something in

118

his voice which told her he was not – entirely indifferent. Then would come sanity, and a violent scolding of herself for being such a fool.

And again and again the thought returned to torment her: How much remained of the love that there had once been between himself and the girl who had so unexpectedly crossed his path again? The memory of that day when Mrs. Tyson had been so upset that she had unguardedly blurted out the story of the past and her fears for the future, was deeply graven on Hilary's unhappy and self-tormented mind. Useless to tell herself that there was nothing more hopeless than unrequited love.

With a great effort she pulled herself together, and attacked the typewriter with an energy that verged on ferocity. Her nurse's training coming to her aid, she resolutely thrust away her unhappy thoughts; and when finally she rose from the desk, the pile of letters and notes completed, the wave of unhappiness which had threatened to engulf her had been resolutely repressed.

Frant had asked her to have tea with herself and John Dallam, and it would do her good. A brisk walk on this lovely sunny afternoon when the gardens of Tarnmere were fragrant with the brief time of blossom, laden with trees of white and purple lilac, and golden showers of laburnum, the stately procession of spring that had opened like a minuet with blackthorn, almond and flowering cherry, some to show like fleeting ghosts in the cold northern breezes – a few hours of loveliness and then no more. But now with warmer weather soon would come the apotheosis of the first roses which even now were putting forth their first tentative buds.

She had just slipped on her linen jacket when the telephone on her desk rang. She picked it up, and Frant's voice came across the wire:

"Hilary? . . . Good. Any chance of you getting off extra early? Because I'm at John's, helping him with a sand-

119

papering job. So if you'd like to look in at the shop you can play foreman of the works and then we'll all go along to my place and put the kettle on nearer tea-time—"

"Fine," Hilary replied. "As it happens, I was just coming along. Maybe John can find me a job to do too."

Frant's delightful chuckle came across the wire. "You've quite enough to do at that typewriter! See you, lovey."

Hilary smiled as she replaced the telephone and went out of the room. For a young woman who protested that she had no thought of marriage where John Dallam was concerned, she certainly seemed, thought Frant's friend while she walked along towards the village, to be seeing a lot of John lately!

As for John – she had an idea that that large young man, for all his quietness, was not without his own brand of shrewd wisdom. He knew when to play a waiting game, and meeting Frant's cheerful friendliness on her own grounds, only gave away his deeper feelings by an occasional hint of possessiveness, none the weaker for being carefully veiled. Hilary often felt he was like a skilful angler playing a difficult catch. What the end might be was still anyone's question, but for the sake of both her friends she could only hope for the best.

When she arrived at the front of the antique shop there was no one to be seen; but a lot of talking and laughter sounded from the small walled yard at the side of the premises. She pushed open a door in the high wall, and recoiled at the pungent smell of paint-stripper. Frant, in one of her most ancient and disgraceful painting smocks and an old pair of jeans, was standing in front of a tall wooden tallboy of drawers and a cupboard, whose graceful lines were apparent even on the stone flags of what John termed his "junk yard", while John himself, in overalls and a smeared khaki shirt, a wad of emery paper in one hand, grinned round at her.

"Sorry to hold up the tea-party," he said. "Another quarter of an hour and I'll do a quick-change act for our glamorous hostess here—" He indicated his beloved, who was also busy, sandpapering with great care a carved wheatsheaf which bordered the cupboard doors.

"Sit down and make yourself at home, ducky," Frant commanded. "John, a sheet of newspaper for Hilary, or she'll mark her skirt on that chair. . . . And for goodness' sake cork that can of paint-stripper now we've done with it. The pong is simply horrible!"

"What on earth have you got there?" Hilary walked round the tallboy, examining it with interest. "Surely that's handcarving?" She ran a finger over the wheat-sheafs which were interspersed with small birds in flight. And then glancing up at the frieze along the top of the cupboard: "Why, is that a marigold I see before me?"

"It is; but you mustn't even misquote Macbeth, or John's business will go up in flames!" Frant returned. "Genuine Adam, no less. John has been days in getting rid of years – and layers of horrible greeny-yellow paint, and I'm helping with the finishing bits before the real work starts of restoring the original polish."

"Not the original," John corrected her. "That went a century or more ago, in the kitchen of the farmhouse at whose sale I picked this up for a couple of quid a few weeks back. Something given to a family retainer on her marriage, no doubt, when the original Big House had no further use for it! You're an observant lass, Hilary: the marigold is genuine, and this is undoubtedly one of the Adam brothers' more solid pieces, suitable for a country gentleman's residence. Mine is only a wild guess, so heaven only knows how it really fetched up at a farm ten miles from anywhere on the other side of Skiddaw!"

"Fascinating!" Hilary exclaimed. "And definitely *not* what Horace Walpole termed 'a gew-gaw and gingerbread snippet of embroidery' – I've often wondered why he disliked the Adams' work so much."

"You wouldn't, if you'd ever been to an exhibition of the monstrosities in Gothic he collected for Strawberry Hill," John replied. "This is quite a find – though of course nothing like the bureau for which, thanks to you, I got such a good sum from the great Mr. Vernon Fairfax. Who has also commissioned me to search for other 'bargains'."

"Talking of the Fairfaxes," Frant observed while she went on sandpapering, "I hear they're giving a grand cocktail party some time soon – apparently a sort of belated housewarming for Hollins Hall."

Hilary made a grimace. "I've heard rumours. I suppose all the grandest in the county will be invited."

"Then as apparently most of the old families have either moved away, died out or been forced to sell, it won't be a very big party, I should think," Frant remarked. "So no doubt Mrs. Fairfax will be forced to lower her social sights somewhat if she wants to make any sort of showing to impress the neighbourhood. I know that's being catty, but I haven't had her for all those sittings – and the portrait's not nearly ready yet – without knowing that one backwards."

"Well, thank goodness I shan't be asked – being a common tradesman," John laughed. "Which is a relief, because I loathe all parties, and most of all cocktail parties. Give me a sing-song and plenty of beer with the lads at the White Lion any old night!"

"John Dallam, you are a low, common person quite unfit for delicate female society!" Frant informed him, her lips primmed but her eyes laughing. "We won't have him to tea after all, will we, Hilary?"

"Perhaps better not." Hilary shook her head, trying to look solemn. "D'you think he drinks from his saucer?"

"Of course I do," John said promptly. "I've been

122

thrown out of Fortnum's, Harrods and the Ritz in Paris for just that. But you still love your low-lifer a little, don't you, Frant darling?"

"Not at all. I'm just sorry for you," his beloved retorted blightingly. "And now shut up and finish your bit, while I do the rest of this border – or poor Hilary will never get any tea this afternoon."

Half an hour later her host and companion, their tasks done and themselves spruced up – which in John's case had meant a disappearance upstairs and entire quick change into blue shirt and slacks – they arrived at Frant's little house.

Opening the gay blue front door, Frant withdrew her latch-key and bent to pick up a large white envelope from the mat.

"Not a bill for once!" she observed. And ripping it open: "Or a cheque either! I'm afraid. Hul-lo! What have we here?" She scanned the expensively embossed, gilt-edged card she held. "Ah! 'An invitation from the Queen, to play croquet'! The frog footman evidently couldn't wait!"

"What *are* you waffling about, my love?" John looked over her shoulder and whistled.

"Champagne cocktails, complete with buffet. 'Mr. and Mrs. Vernon Fairfax request the pleasure of Miss Veronica Frant's company on the 17th.' Oh well – anyway, the drinks are bound to be good."

"Rather you than me," Hilary remarked. "And that is anything but sour grapes."

"Don't be too sure you won't be asked!" Frant's smile held a glint of mischief. "I've been having all sorts of questions asked about people whose families have been in Tarnmere for centuries! And while we're about it, the glamorous Lena has discovered your dark secret, John – that you're cousin to a belted Earl, even though very distant! Antique dealers have become, in the opinion of

123

Mrs. Fairfax, '*quite* different from other people who keep shops. Really *top* persons go in for it all over the country – look at the Grosvenor House Fair and Chelsea!' So I don't mind betting you'll be in for it, my lad."

"Oh, no!" John looked horrified, and Hilary said:

"Well, one can always find a polite excuse and refuse, I suppose. Anyway, as mere secretary to the doctor that worry won't arise for me!"

But she was wrong. When she arrived home after the gay little tea party and entering the hallway to the accompaniment of old Shep's welcome, her eyes fell on a large square white envelope lying on the shining Jacobean oak table, and a pang of dismay shot through her.

Tearing it open, she already knew what it contained, and was scanning it in growing dismay when Cousin Priscilla came through from the kitchen.

"Is that an invitation card to the party everyone's saying they're going to give at Hollins Hall?" she asked, and as Hilary nodded: "Well! What excitement – may I see?" And as the card was handed to her: "A champagne cocktail party, with buffet. My, how grand! I'm glad they've had the courtesy to ask you, love."

"I'm not," Hilary said flatly. "And somehow I must find a polite excuse not to go—"

"Not to go? For goodness' sake, why?" Cousin Priscilla stared at her in surprise. It's not the sort of thing I'd care for myself. I'd get tiddly!" Her jolly laugh rang out. "But it will liven things up a bit for you. It's little enough fun *you've* had since you came back from that hospital."

But being Mrs. Fairfax's guest was not Hilary's idea of fun. Considering that on the only occasions they had met, Lena had been very cool and distant, she could not understand in the least why she should have been invited, and had no wish to accept hospitality in order to make a larger background for the people whom Lena in her shallow snobbishness considered really "mattered".

But Mrs. Brathay made short work of her young cousin's determination to refuse, and said stringently:

"I've never heard such a lot of nonsense! Never mind how high and mighty Mrs. Fairfax may be, she's not the only one giving the party, and you may be sure that Vernon Fairfax will be very hurt if you don't go. His family knew yours long before you were born – that's why you and Tim have been asked, for sure. You can't be rude enough to snub Vernon just because you don't care for his wife!"

"But—" Hilary paused, then gave a rather rueful laugh. "I suppose there's something in what you say, Priscilla, but – Oh well, I'll have to sleep on it and think it over. I don't want to appear rude—"

"Well, that's just what you'd be doing if you refused," Cousin Priscilla interrupted.

Hilary glanced at the card again. "Anyway, this invitation includes Tim and I'm quite sure he'll want to back out."

Unexpectedly, when her brother arrived in later that evening, he was not so reluctant at the idea of going to Hollins Hall as Hilary had expected.

"Priscilla's right, you know," he said. "Considering Fairfax's people and ours were friends heaven knows how long ago, it won't do to appear discourteous, Sis. Besides," he added with a grin, "I must confess to a curiosity to see the great Mrs. Fairfax in all her glory! Remember I haven't yet met her, though I've glimpsed her in the village, and she looks quite a dish. And I believe Fairfax isn't such a bad sort, tycoon or not."

Hilary had forgotten her brother's incorrigible bachelor propensities for taking an interest in any good-looking girl who might appear on his horizon; so it was with some considerable annoyance that she realised her determination to get out of going to Lena Fairfax's housewarming was not possible.

And when on her arriving in the office next morning she discovered that Blake had received an invitation and intended to accept it, she did not know whether to feel glad or sorry that she would be there. Somehow she would have expected him to refuse. Did his acceptance mean that he and Lena were better friends? However stupid it might be, the idea strengthened the nagging pain in her heart, even with the memory of Mrs. Tyson's words that she was now sure any feeling Blake had ever felt for Lena Fairfax was definitely "over and done with".

The housekeeper continued to be comforting, while bringing in tea and biscuits for the mid-morning break.

"The thing worried me at first when it came," Nannie Tyson confided, "but when Mr. Blake said in such a bored voice that 'he couldn't not go without appearing impolite', it was easy to see he meant just what he said; and that there's nothing left of the old folly where either of them are concerned. For which I can thank the good Lord, and see him off to this grand party with an easy mind!"

Mrs. Tyson's words might not only express her own ease of mind, and also have the power to lighten Hilary's sore heart. But it was as well for them both that they could not guess, that however indifferent Blake might be, things were inclined to be somewhat different where Lena herself was concerned.

When, on her husband's return from his latest business trip, Lena had told him of her intention to hold a "house-warming" and shown him a list of the intended guests, he had approved, kissing her indulgently.

"A good idea, darling. High time we did something of the sort." And then seeing Blake's name his smile faded, and he observed, after a short pause in which Lena watched him covertly: "I see you've got Blake Kinross down. Is that absolutely necessary?"

"What, the local doctor? Of course I had to ask him. Surely you're not still being silly about Blake?" she

126

demanded. "You stupid old thing!" She patted his face. "It would look like a deliberate affront to leave him out."

"I suppose so," he admitted grudgingly. "But—"

"Oh, Vernon my pet!" she said impatiently. "Just how stupid can you be? Because of something that happened and was done with years ago, you're still jealous. It must be a guilt complex because I let you steal me! Darling, *do* be your age!"

"That, my dear," he said drily but with a glint of sardonic humour, "is not exactly a tactful request under the circumstances."

"You great big silly!" She ruffled his greying hair. "You look wonderful for your age – which I never think about. But if you're going to start your old jealousy of Blake Kinross, I shall think you in your second childhood!"

"In that case, invite the fellow," he answered with a shrug of his big shoulders and a half smile that softened as she kissed him. And then holding her to him in an arm the muscles of which were like iron he kissed her back with a sudden fierce passion: "If I'm a fool sometimes, it's because I love you so much – never forget that."

"Why should I ever, darlingest?" But though she returned his kisses readily, through her closed eyes came the vision of another face; rugged, good-looking and disturbingly attractive to her mind and her shallow heart. A picture she had prudently tried to put from her, but which yet remained tantalisingly liable to crop up at unexpected moments. Somehow just lately she had thought it might be better if she had not met Blake Kinross again. But never in her sublime assurance did the thought come to her that in finding more than she had at first thought of the old attraction left, she might be playing with fire. A fire, that though she little dreamed it, could have the power to flame into a searing danger threatening the happiness of not only her own, but other lives as well.

127

CHAPTER NINE

The door of Hollins Hall stood hospitably open to the moonlit softness of the summer evening, and the long windows of the great drawing-room sent a golden glow out over the terraced gardens, while skilful floodlighting heightened the effect of flowering trees and shrubs in the grounds. A sound of lilting music echoed romantically into the deepening dusk, and servants with drink-laden trays wound their way deftly through the crowds of gay chattering guests who thronged not only the drawing-room, but the adjoining apartments as well.

Lena, exquisitely gowned in a cocktail dress of jade green and gold brocade, had only recently released her husband from her side. There were still a few guests to greet, but now she had time to survey the colourful scene before her with supreme satisfaction. She had not even begun to anticipate the least failure, but it was gratifying that not one of her more important invitations had been declined. She guessed cynically that where the County was concerned, curiosity quite as much as the prospect of unlimited champagne had brought them here; though what mattered was that they *were* here – in force.

Major-General Sir Arthur Blakeney with his tall and somewhat awe-inspiring spouse was talking to Miss Aurelia and Miss Maria Skelwith, two elderly maiden sisters famous for their outspoken comments and caustic opinions on everything from local farming (in which they were experts) to world affairs. Admiral Vane, stocky, white-haired and distinguished, with a sailor's far-seeing blue gaze, deceptively fierce, for he was a jolly old sea-dog with a great sense of humour, had turned up with his more austere sister who looked after him with a devotion worthy of a Dorothy Wordsworth, seemed to be thoroughly enjoying themselves; and even old Mr. Vereker from Marsdale Grange had not failed, and that was indeed a triumph, for of late years he had become something of a recluse. This evening he was cackling with laughter amid a bevy of younger female guests who seemed to relish his Edwardian naughtiness as they would have done a piece of John Dallam's antique furniture. Mr. Vereker was reputed to be enormously rich, though for ever lamenting incipient poverty, and lived in a hideous Victorian mansion on a hillside overlooking the lake, surrounded by a number of servants reminiscent of half a century ago. An eccentric bachelor, he was the last of a very old Tarnmere family if one excluded a farming cousin of the same name in New Zealand.

All very satisfactory, Lena decided, as her eyes went to Frant, very elegant this evening in a suit of turquoise wild silk that suited her to perfection. Dear Frant! thought Lena, with just the slightest little pull of self-doubt. So refreshingly astringent and forthright – if the thought occurred that one could not always be sure whether a hint of acid sometimes lay behind her smiling and always cordial sessions with her sitter, it was easy to push it to one side.

Then Lena glanced towards where another group of young men surrounded a girl in a simple dress of some softly draping mauve material which set off her auburn hair and the creamy oval of her face to perfection. Hilary made a charming picture, poised and quite unselfconscious, but that was one which gave Lena no satisfaction at all, and for an instant a crease appeared between her golden brows, while her smiling lips tightened before she turned to a late arrival.

If she had had her way Hilary Talgarth would certainly not have been here tonight; but Vernon's acquaintance with the family at Willowbeck, and the fact that the girl and her brother were so obviously socially acceptable, had made it impossible to ignore the Talgarths. And certainly Tim Talgarth, tall and handsome in an accustomed dark suit, was quite an acquisition in himself, going down particularly well with the female guests, and very popular with the men. John Dallam too, towering head and shoulders over nearly every other man present; the discovery that besides being so friendly with Frant, he was distantly related to a personage whom Frant herself had irreverently described as "a belted Earl" gave him added value in Lena's odiously snobbish opinion.

Only Frant guessed, maliciously smiling across at him, just how much John was disliking the whole affair. But she guessed that a few more glasses of the deceptively potent drink being offered around – many of which the ladies present wisely declined, sticking to milder fruit-cups – he would cheer up and begin to enjoy himself!

But the evening was so far spoiled for Lena; until the sudden arrival of her very latest guest caused her eyes to light up. She crossed over to the tall figure who had just entered the crowded room, and said lightly:

"Hullo there! So glad you could make it after all, Blake."

Conscious of her husband's eyes watching her, she refrained from her first impulse to extend both her hands, and instead gave him one which he took briefly, apologising for his lateness.

"I thought you were going back on your word, so proving yourself my only failure," she murmured.

"No. I said I would come," he replied. Then, his glance going round the throng of laughing, chattering guests: "What a very successful party, to be sure! You're to be congratulated, Lena."

"All my parties are successful – aren't they, Vernon?" She turned her head as her husband came up. "The doctor has actually found time to come after all, my dear—"

"How are you, Kinross?" Vernon's handclasp was brief, his voice forcedly cordial. "No doubt you've had a tiring day and will be glad of a drink. Here –" He beckoned to a white-coated manservant who approached with a tray of champagne cocktails. Blake accepted one, and as the Fairfaxes were claimed by other guests, made his way through the crowd towards Hilary.

Catching sight of him, she was aware once more of those quickened heartbeats, the knowledge that he was around bringing that strange breathlessness. A moment before she too had been wondering if he would turn up.

"You're late," she said, foolishly pleased to hear how normal her voice sounded.

"An unexpected telephone call from Liverpool – one of the big men about a medical conference next week," he answered. "You look very charming tonight, Hilary – or I should say, perhaps, a shade more charming than usual."

The compliment was so unexpected that she flushed scarlet, furious with herself for doing so, then managed to regain her poise and say lightly:

"Thank you, kind sir. And it *is* kind when one knows oneself far outshone by so many here."

"Nonsense. I'm never kind," he returned. "It's no more than the truth . . . Ah, good evening, Miss Aurelia. How are the azaleas this year? More to your satisfaction than last time, I hope?"

"Flourishing, thank heaven – like myself, dear man!" Miss Aurelia Skelwith, enormously stout, rather red in the face and beaming, dug the doctor playfully in the ribs. "Not often we meet, I'm afraid. But m'sister and myself hardly ever have a day's bad health – disgraceful for the last of our family, ain't it? Rotten patients, eh! Never make your fortune."

"Why don't you come and dine, dear man?" Miss Maria joined them, a thin edition of the elder Skelwith. "Of course you're worked off your feet." She smiled at Hilary,

131

who would tactfully have moved away. "Hullo! Hilary, my child, you're lookin' very nice tonight. Just seen that brother of yours and had a chat about the new Jerseys I've bought. Glad to hear things are flourishin' at Willowbeck – but then I can't remember a time when they ever did anything else! Excellent farmers, all the Talgarths!"

"Thank you –" Hilary began, struggling to keep a straight face as Miss Aurelia broke in robustly: "No better farmin' stock in all this part of the world. Older family than ours, y'know. And it mustn't be allowed to die out!" She gave Hilary a friendly but piercing stare. "Time that brother of yours married and carried on the line! When's he goin' to stop playing around as a bachelor and get himself a wife, eh?"

"I really don't know. But I'm sure he'll find someone before too long – considering the eye he has to pretty girls someone's bound to take him off me sooner or later," Hilary replied, unable to keep back her laughter.

"Then he'd better make it sooner!" Miss Aurelia advised, and her sister nodded agreement, adding: "And what about yourself, m'dear? High time *you* found yourself a nice young feller to marry. You may tell an old bachelor girl like m'self not to butt in, but neither Aurelia or I were ever of the marrying kind. You are – and with those looks it'd be sheer wickedness to waste yourself. Don't you 'gree?" She turned to Blake.

"Certainly," he said gravely. "But don't encourage her – she's useful!" Though his eyes were twinkling there was a warmth behind his smiling glance, and Miss Aurelia's glance, already piercing, became suddenly gimlet-like. But all she said was:

"Humph! Well, we'll wait and see, eh?" And changing the subject, enabled Hilary, aware of hot cheeks, to drift away to where Frant was standing.

"And what is the cause of that delightful Victorian shell-pink blush?" enquired her friend. She looked across

132

to where the Skelwith ladies still held Blake in animated conversation. "If you've been talking to Aurelia and Maria Skelwith, I can guess they've been their usual forthright selves! Telling you to marry and have a large family, no doubt?"

"They think Tim ought to stop being a bachelor, and marry 'to carry on the line' without further ado!"

"Good lord! Give the poor chap a bit of time!" Frant exclaimed. "I sometimes think the motto of this age ought to be 'Marry too early, repent before thirty', but it's all a matter of opinion." Unconsciously her gaze rested on John's tall figure.

"Perhaps. But it's also a shade unkind to keep hanging around too long – under some circumstances," Hilary told her drily.

Frant shrugged her slender shoulder. "I've told you already, ducky, and I'm not going to again. So far as John and myself are concerned – well, we'll just see." She changed the subject rather abruptly. "That brother of yours seems to be having a whale of a time. Surrounded by pretty girls. I don't think the Skelwith ladies have much to worry about there."

And certainly Tim, having imbibed an already quite judicious quantity of champagne, was thoroughly enjoying himself. Later, when many of the guests had drifted into the long room where a magnificent buffet was laden with every delicacy suitable to such an occasion, he came up to his sister and asked:

"Do you mind if I go on with Carswells, love? We've just had a glorious tuck-in, and now with our hostess's kind permission, they're continuing with an impromptu dance at their place, and they've asked me along. I'll leave the car, so you can drive yourself home – if you'll be O.K.?"

"I like that!" his sister retorted indignantly. "I'd far rather trust myself at the wheel than you! Certainly go, and get someone else to drive *you* home – unless you feel a nice long midnight walk would be more in order.''

Tim cocked an eye at her. "Madam, are you suggesting I can't carry my drink?"

"Not exactly, but I know you," she said affectionately. "Go and enjoy yourself – I'll get myself back."

Blake who, unnoticed by brother and sister, was standing near, turned a not very approving glance on Tim. "I'll drive Hilary home," he announced.

She glanced round quickly. "How kind of you, but—"

"No 'buts'. And you take your sister's advice, young man. If you drive, drive carefully. Roberts has quite enough to do now the tourists are beginning to be on the rampage again."

"Honestly, I shan't need a breathalyser." Tim's laugh was a little sheepish. "But thanks a lot – if you'll look after the lass—"

"I'll look after her."

"Then we'll step off," Tim told his sister. "Goodnight. I won't forget." He grinned at Blake more confidently. "Doctor's orders!" But though he was still smiling as he moved off, his grey eyes were thoughtful. He had teased Hilary about her employer more than once, but this time it seemed to him that there was a certain note of possession in Blake Kinross's tone. He was wondering suddenly if things had gone – well, further than he had guessed. However, whatever might have happened in that direction was entirely his sister's affair . . . .

Meanwhile she was protesting, "I really don't want to take you out of your way, Doctor. John Dallam will give me a lift—"

"John will doubtless be driving Miss Frant," Blake interrupted. "Don't be a spoilsport. Three is *not* company!"

"Oh!" Her eyes widened, and then they were both laughing together. The sound made an infectiously pleasant duet, but Lena Fairfax, looking across from where she was hemmed in by a bevy of admiring males, found it anything but pleasing.

For Lena the evening had been an unending triumph; though having, like the good hostess she was, constantly to circulate, she had had far too little time to spend with the one guest in whom she was most interested. And it had afforded her no pleasure whatever when she had seen Blake squire Hilary Talgarth into the buffet, taking such obvious pleasure in the girl's company.

Her vague dislike of Hilary, hitherto pushed to the back of her mind, had crystallised and hardened this evening; and when she came across them much later out on the paved terrace beyond the open glass doors, her eyes were glittering with something less pleasant than the champagne she had imbibed. Their encounter with the Skelwith ladies, too, had not escaped her notice; neither had the fact that those self-same elderly sisters had accorded her no more than the formal politeness of most of the more exalted guests in this gathering. It seemed that the Talgarth girl was popular with everyone – Sir Arthur Blakeney and Admiral Vane had flirted with her in an unexceptional, elderly-gentlemanly way; and even Lady Blakeney, a high-nosed matron who might have been expected to pay scant attention to the daughter of a statesman farmer, however long the family had been in Tarnmere, was exceptionally gracious. Ever quick to sense social nuances, Lena had swiftly realised that "that receptionist girl", as she termed her in her own mind, was on a more secure footing here tonight than the great Mrs. Fairfax herself. So it was in a determinedly gay but somewhat high voice that she accosted Blake:

"Hello, you! I've been wanting to get hold of you. I'm afraid someone else will have to look after Miss Talgarth – you don't mind, do you?" She just glanced at Hilary. "But I've been so busy I haven't had time to even get near the

135

buffet and I'm starving. But now there's a very special little supper laid on—"

If she had not had just a little too much champagne she would not have betrayed herself into such obvious bad taste. Beside her Hilary felt Blake stiffen, but he answered smilingly:

"I'm so sorry, but I'm afraid we must leave your delightful party. I'm quite certain there are a score of your guests eager to be your escort. But unfortunately there's work to be done early tomorrow, so I'm motoring Hilary back, and I'm afraid it's really time for us to say goodbye and thank you."

Although she had coloured at Lena's insufferable rudeness, seeing her hostess's almost outraged expression Hilary had a quite schoolgirlish longing to giggle. Lena was for once utterly disconcerted, and realising she had made a *gaffe*, hastened to retrieve her position.

"Oh, don't go yet – either of you. Look," she leaned forward, putting an impulsive hand on Blake's arm, "we can – easily make room for Miss Talgarth. Do stay." The invitation cost her as much effort as the brilliantly false smile she flashed at Hilary.

"My dear Lena," Blake protested, "how you can even mention such a word as supper after your princely refreshments I don't know. Thank you very much, but we really must be going. A doctor's life is not his own, and unfortunately poor Hilary gets caught up too."

"Oh, it's nothing more than chicken salad or a strip of smoked salmon with asparagus," she assured him. "Just an excuse to prolong a rather nice evening." And then, meeting his polite but inflexible smile: "Oh, very well!" She turned to Hilary. "Don't let yourself be bullied into going early! Won't you at least stay a little longer? Please do."

Her own smile equalling the falseness of the one fixed on her, Hilary shook her head. "I really must be getting home – I have to be up horribly early. Thank you for the loveliest evening . . . Oh, there's your husband. I must thank him too."

She turned to where Vernon Fairfax was standing nearby, surveying them with a rather sardonic expression, which melted into a warm smile as she held out her hand to him. After that there was nothing for Lena to do, but accept their farewells gracefully, aware of Vernon's satisfaction as he watched Blake escort Hilary out.

"You know, I believe there's a bit of a case there," he told his wife, perhaps not entirely unconscious of hidden annoyance he was causing. "That's a dear child—".

Biting back an almost overwhelming desire to tell him vulgarly to "Shut up!", Lena walked away, her mouth set into a hard line. The memory of Blake escorting Hilary Talgarth out into the night rankled. Good heavens! what had the girl got to interest him? Passable looks, a certain flair for wearing inexpensive clothes, a poise that was rather out of place in a person of her position! . . . Oh well, best forget her entirely, after all she couldn't be less important.

Which was why it was all the more infuriating that that memory remained, spoiling all her triumph in the success of her party.

Although it was only late May, the Lakeland night, lit by a full moon, was fragrant with the scent of the first roses. The reluctant spring seemed far enough away to belong to another world, and only on the highest peaks did the line of rapidly melting snows remain to presage another possible cooler spell. But now it was warm enough almost for high summer, and Hilary hardly needed the light wrap which covered her dress. The glow of light and sounds of music from the great house lay behind them now, and ahead stretched Tarnmere Lake, glimmering and mysterious with the moonlight reflected on darkened waters.

The little island in the centre possessed a small white building, the whim of some Georgian squire who had made the Grand Tour, and built a summer pavilion to which his guests could be rowed out on such nights as this.

"Probably with a boatload of musicians dutifully entertaining with Mr. Handel's Water Music," Blake commented while he slowed the car down to a crawl, letting them drink in the beauty of the scene. Surveying it with a little sigh of satisfaction, looking up at the surrounding hills, their jagged peaks romantic silhouettes against the star-strewn sky, Hilary quoted softly:

" 'Earth hath not anything to show more fair' – and yet when he wrote that Wordsworth didn't mean his own beloved Lakeland, but London on an early summer's morning."

"He could hardly have written as much now if he'd seen the moneygrabbing and greed – the ruin wrought by property developers, whom Dante would certainly have put in one of the lowest circles of his Inferno!" said Blake. "But even now when I have occasion to cross that same bridge on a summer's morning, London has still not lost that certain enchantment despite everything man can do to try and ruin it. I was there a few weeks ago, and in the spring light the curve of London river, St. Paul's dwarfed but still its lovely self, that 'madrigal in stone' with the Tower in the distance – still one glimpses something of what moved that tiresome old man to write his immortal sonnet."

She nodded. "I think I know what you mean. I once dreamed of finally fetching up at one of the London hospitals," she said a little wistfully.

He looked round, slowing down still further. "Do you still hanker after a nursing career?" he asked gently.

She shook her head with a rueful smile. "What's the use? After all, I'm very happy to be back here where I was born. And I like my job."

He brought the car to a halt. "Do you, Hilary – really?"

It was her turn to look at him, and though his face was no more than a profile in the dimness of the shaded road, her heart was suddenly beating faster – that foolish, unmanageable heart. She told him simply: "Without it I should have been desolate; especially in those first months when I could only think of myself as a failure—"

"Of course you weren't a failure," he said rather sharply. "I happen to know your Principal Nursing Officer – Miss Jevons – and she told me she had a young nurse from my part of the world who, if her health hadn't given way, would have made one of the best Sisters she could ever have hoped for. That, though I haven't told you this before, was one of the reasons I lost no time in roping you in for the job. And it's obvious enough that you're well and strong now, even though you could never go back to a city environment—'

"Oh!" She stared at him in startled surprise. "How kind of Miss Jevons—"

"Well, I have every reason to be grateful to her," he observed. She knew that he was smiling, and told him rather breathlessly:

"I'm glad I've proved – satisfactory!"

"Satisfactory!" He repeated the word almost explosively, and with a quick touch stopped the car engine. "You're far more than that!" And as she was silent, the thudding of her heart seeming like thunder in the stillness of the night, he turned fully towards her and taking her hands, drew her closer, bending his face to hers. "You've become so – indispensable that I want to make sure I shall never lose you – my darling!"

The next instant she was in his arms, and his lips were warm and demanding against her own. All the weeks of longing and desolate dreams she had tried so firmly to control melted into oblivion with the sweet reality of that kiss. The moon and the stars seemed to shimmer into a golden chain of light, drawing them ever closer in the ecstasy of those magic moments while her lips surrendered to the unbelievable sweetness of the unspoken words on his.

Melting into his embrace, she seemed to dwell in a lover's eternity. Then sanity returned, and she drew back with a little cry that was half a sob. His arms slackened instantly, but did not break their encirclement of her slender body. She said unsteadily:

"Blake – Oh, this can't be true! You can't really love me—"

"But, my sweet and darling idiot, haven't I just shown you clearly how much I do?" There was a tremor in his own voice. "I love you, love you, love you. And have done for weeks – I think ever since that night when we worked so late on Cowbiggin Hill in that driving cold and rain. I knew then that I'd found the only girl who can ever be anything in my life – the one girl whom I can't live without!"

"Oh! And I didn't think you could ever care for me! I loved you so much – and I was so unhappy!" she confessed. "I tried to tell myself what a fool I was being." She put a hand to touch his cheek, and he caught and kissed it. "Now I can't believe that this is really happening."

"Well, it is. And what is also going to happen is that we'll be married at the soonest possible moment! What a wonderful bit of excitement for the village! They'll turn up at the church to a woman – and a man as well," he answered, kissing her again. And then: "Anyway, I don't have to warn *you* of the hazards of being a doctor's wife! All the same, my sweet," it was his turn to draw back, looking down at her with grave eyes, "it is a lot to ask, even of yourself, who know just what it all means! Hours at all odds, disturbed nights, spoiled meals, sudden dislocation of plans social or domestic. And on top of that a somewhat impatient and at times uncertain-tempered devil

140

like myself! Do you think you can really put up with all that, my darling, and survive?"

"Who's talking nonsense now?" She kissed his cheek, and then when she was able to recover her breath: "What does anything – what can anything matter so long as we have each other – and that I'm sure of your love? You see –" her voice wavered a moment, "on that night of the bus accident I saw your face when the Fairfaxes' car stopped. And then quite by chance I – learned a little of what had happened in the past, and I felt sure you—" She broke off as his arm tightened about her.

"When I first met Lena again, I had a shock – it was only natural," he told her. "But after a very little while – in fact, that next day at John Dallam's place – I knew, to put it unchivalrously, what an escape the young and callow Blake Kinross had had. I'll bet," he laughed softly, "Nannie Tyson got in a flap and confided in you – so you needn't tell me! Well, she had no need to worry, and you can forget it all as completely as I have."

He paused a moment. "But before you do so, I'll tell you this: I thought myself badly hurt at the time, but afterwards I realised that what I'd felt had only been – well, the kind of infatuation the Lenas of this world cause – infatuation and no more. It took a far different girl, worlds removed in sweetness and loveliness, to capture my heart – now and for ever."

"Oh, Blake, my darling." Her shining auburn hair was against his breast, the pounding of his heart under her cheek. "I can't believe in so much happiness! I only know I—" She stopped and he said, his mouth muffled in her hair:

"Go on, say it! It's not all that difficult!"

"I love you – quite desperately! Now and always!" Her arms going up about his neck, she drew his face down to hers, and once again time stood still, and the world was narrowed into the circle of their love.

CHAPTER TEN

OF course Frant was the first person to be told – except Tim, who had accepted the news with unexpected enthusiasm.

"I'm glad for you both, Hilary darling," he announced, kissing her with unusual fervour. "I'm not at all sure your betrothed looks on your little brother with the enthusiasm my undoubted talents merit, but I'm more than ready to welcome him as a brother-in-law, and so you may inform him. But all I want is your happiness—"

This somewhat unexpected acceptance of the situation had caused Hilary to shed unexpected tears. Which were dissipated by a brotherly buffet, and Cousin Priscilla, in floods of pleasurable tears herself, that she had to be informed were quite out of place and unnecessary!

As for the village, the announcement of the engagement between Hilary Talgarth and Doctor Blake Kinross was received with universal delight and acclaim; and a shower of good wishes that was almost overwhelming.

But before anyone else knew Frant had been told after a walk up to Heron Tarn above the foaming waters of Armboth Ghyll that fell in a seven-hundred-foot milky white cascade into the jade green depths of the pool that fed the rippling beck winding below the towering heights of Appleriggin Crag.

When Hilary broke the news the two girls were standing on a ledge of rock that gave a breathtaking view of the valley below; away to the left lay the dark waters of the tarn which, true to its name, showed a solitary heron standing meditatively on one leg as though pondering some abstruse mathematical problem. Cloud shadows dappled the grey-walled meadows on the lower slopes where the Herdwicks raised black, incurious faces lit by their so unexpectedly lovely amber eyes to the small, distant figures of the girls in the coloured dresses far above.

For a moment Frant stared, then with a cry of delight hugged Hilary delightedly.

"Darling Hilary, could anything be more heaven! Bless you, my infant – and dear Blake too. Not," she added, "that I haven't seen this coming along for some time. You two have, in Shakespeare's words, been 'smelling of April and May', especially during these last weeks."

"That's more than I could have told," Hilary retorted. "I believed he didn't give me a thought! While I – Oh, Frant, I've been so desperately unhappy knowing how much I loved him while I was sure he was – just wrapped up in his work."

"Ducky, how stupid can you get? And how true it is that the most trite clichés can be apt on occasion: 'Love is blind'; 'The Little Blind God'! No wonder highbrows sneer at romance, poor dears! Because all the fundamental things of our existence on this planet – life, birth, death – and love, are all alike in being obvious. And your true serious intellectual (a being so often without intelligence) only cares for the over-elaborate and distorted. Which is one of the main reasons society is in such a mess today. But heaven be praised—" Frant laughed suddenly. "Just listen to me! Anyway, thank heaven for people like you and your young man who can still fall in love, just in the way it should be! And when, may I ask, is the wedding to be?"

"As soon as possible. In the church here, of course." Hilary looked across to where the square, part Saxon, part Norman tower of the ancient grey church showed like a toy amid a group of billowing elms in the midst of the village.

"I shall come and weep violently in a back pew with John to support me," Frant announced. "You mightn't think it, but I adore crying at weddings – especially when one knows they're not the kind one knows have a more than fifty-fifty chance of ending up in the divorce courts in anything from two to five years!"

"You won't be in a back pew at all, but in your rightful place near the bride," Hilary corrected, adding mischievously: "It's not poor John's fault that you're not able to act as matron of honour!"

"Pooh!" This time it was Frant's cheeks that were pink. "Tell me – is Tim pleased?"

"Very happy for me, but a little bit dashed, I'm afraid, though he says it was 'only to be expected', having been an onlooker like yourself! He says he'll be a lone, lorn bachelor with only Cousin Priscilla to look after him – (she's in the seventh heaven, of course!) as if she won't do that as well as she's always done. Anyway, I've an idea he won't be 'lone' for long, because he's always around with the prettiest of the Carswell sisters – the one who got up that dance following the Fairfax party. Mary Carswell is a sweet thing, so I'm hoping for the best."

It was not until some days after this mountainside conversation that the village learned of the engagement, to the excited delight of the many who had known the doctor's prospective bride since she was knee-high.

"Aye, and before that," Mr. Hardisty beamed. "And now you're getting a real man! Well, my arthritis won't let me dance at your wedding, but I can still pull a bell rope, and a mighty peal we'll give you both!"

Only Lena, learning the news from her maid with a definite, far from pleasant shock, failed to wish the couple happiness. On the contrary, though, Vernon Fairfax approved wholeheartedly.

"So Kinross is getting married to that charming girl," he said. "Hope he appreciates his luck." And as she was silent he looked up sharply from the local paper he was reading. "Don't you agree, my dear?"

"Why, yes, of course I do." Lena smothered a yawn behind one slender hand. "Though I'm afraid I could be hardly less interested, darling. For someone with as little ambition as poor Blake, no doubt the Talgarth girl will be an ideal wife. However, that's up to him."

"Quite." Again Vernon Fairfax gave his wife a keen glance. "Personally, I think the girl has both looks and character – but you were never very inclined to be generous to your own sex, Lena. I can't think why, when you're so ornamental yourself. Not sour grapes, by any chance?"

She flushed, the quiet sarcasm of his words stinging harder than she liked. There were times when Vernon's ruthless penetration of her inmost self had the power to raise a seething anger in her. But now, as so often before, she was clever enough not to let that annoyance show, and merely shrugged indifferently. "That's a merely foolish suggestion, darling, I'm sorry if I can't get up the requisite enthusiasm – which I'm sure must be by now surging through the entire neighbourhood – anyway," she winced suddenly, "I'm feeling rather under the weather today."

"What's wrong?" He put down the paper, looking across at her with instant concern.

"Pains – rather nasty ones. They kept me awake, and I feel sickish and keep on getting these wretched little stabs. I must have eaten the wrong thing, or something." She placed a hand on her right side. "However, I expect it'll soon go off."

"You've complained of something like that before." His worst enemy could not have accused Fairfax, for all his ruthlessness, of ever being indifferent to his wife's well-being, and a shadow of anxiety appeared in his hard eyes. "If it goes on I'll take you down to London and have you overhauled in Harley Street—"

"Oh, nonsense," she assured him. "It's nothing." She

smiled at him. "Don't look so worried – I think I've been a bit tired since that hectic party. I'll probably have a lie-in tomorrow, and be as right as rain."

"And that is the lot for today, I think, Doctor!" Hilary put a pile of typed letters and neatly clipped sheaf of notes on the desk beside which Blake was standing.

"So it is," he replied. "Which leaves us, as soon as I've signed these, with time to attend to ourselves. I was thinking of a spot of dinner at the Old England – or if you'd rather go further afield than Windermere—"

"I don't mind where I dine, or where we go – so long as it's with you," she told him, and was caught in the strong circle of his arms.

"My sweet delight!" he said a little unsteadily. "In the words of a very old and corny musical comedy song:

'You're adorable—
So adorable.
Quite the nicest girl I've ever found—'"

"I'm glad to hear it!" She linked her arms round his neck. "Incidentally, Doctor Kinross, your hair grows in a most delightful way – which is the most absurd detail to turn a silly girl's heart to water—"

"How very flattering of you, ma'am!" He laughed down at her. "Wouldn't you prefer me to grow it fashionably to my shoulders à la Richard the Third?"

"Heaven forbid! And so, I should think, would the B.M.A.!" she retorted, stroking the thick tawny-streaked hair which had, in spite of all the brushing it received, a tendency to a slight wave.

"Ah! Will you still love me when it starts to go back and I'm finally bald?" he teased.

"Always! And anyway, that's a long way off, we trust!" she told him. "Will *you* still love me when I have to fight off wrinkles and my own hair has grey in it?"

"Always – always!" he repeated, kissing her again. "'Love is not love which alters when it alteration finds'. . . . Damn that telephone. If it's an emergency to spoil our dining out tonight, I'll swear like a trooper. . . . Doctor Kinross speaking."

He had released her and turned to the desk, lifting the telephone off its cradle.

Watching him, she saw the happiness die out of his face to be replaced by the keen, alert attention which told her how in an instant the doctor had taken over from the man.

"Yes? . . . I see. When did the pains start? . . . Some weeks ago, recurring more frequently during this last one. . . . Very well, don't panic. I'll be coming straight over. . . . Yes, within ten minutes."

He replaced the telephone and turned back to Hilary, his face grave. "Bang goes our evening, my sweet. That was Vernon Fairfax in what may fairly be described as a hell of a flap! His wife was taken very ill half an hour ago. He was out, and returned to find the servants rushing around like a lot of frightened hens – none of them apparently having had the sense to ring me. She has violent pains and sickness. Her legs now drawn up, and she seems hardly to know him. Sounds like a classic flaring appendix." He was already half way across the room, bending to pick up his case.

Hilary followed him swiftly. "Shall I stay here by the telephone, or shall I come with you? If arrangements have to be made for an emergency operation, wouldn't it be better for me to be on the spot?"

He considered a moment, then nodded briefly. "It would save time if you came. If she's as bad as she sounds, there's not a second to be wasted."

Moments later they were in the car and he was driving along the road round the lake at reckless speed. Hilary said:

"I suppose Mr. Fairfax will want the best nursing home – though she'd be just as well off in the private wing of any of the local hospitals. After all, if it is appendix, any good surgeon can deal with it promptly—"

"No doubt. But if I know anything of Fairfax he'll be wanting to send to the top M.S. stratum in London," Blake observed rather grimly. "And as there's not likely to be any time for fancy frills he'll have to do as he's told for once in his life." He was silent a moment, his long, capable hands guiding the car deftly round a sharp bend in the road. "With luck – unless he's had to leave unexpectedly – Sir Keith Lowson, who as you know is one of the top men in Liverpool, is staying in Windermere at the Old England – that was why I was thinking of our going there tonight, so that I could show you off to him. . . . No doubt if he's still there, he'd be good enough to break his holiday. In which case Fairfax *would* be in luck. However, first we'll see if all this is the exaggeration of panic."

"From the sound of it I rather doubt that," Hilary commented, and he nodded. Then they were turning in through the wrought-iron gates and up the steeply sloping drive to Hollins Hall.

"Shall I wait here?" she asked as he extricated himself deftly, and took his case.

"If you would. If there has to be a lot of telephoning and the usual procedure, I'll have someone come out for you." He smiled at her, and the next moment was entering the house, the front door of which had been opened by the elderly and tonight agitated-looking butler.

Hilary sat staring through the windscreen at a bed of flowering shrubs immediately in front of her, her hands clasping and unclasping in her lap. The memory of what might have been a lovely evening flitted across her mind, bringing a rueful little smile to her lips. She was learning (as if she hadn't already known!) just what it would be like to be a doctor's wife, even before the knot was tied! And then at the thought of the woman lying in one of those palatial rooms above, seriously perhaps even dangerously ill, her own training came to her, and she forgot all thought of self. Somehow, something inside her told her this was a real emergency, and no false alarm. So she was not surprised when a bare ten minutes later the butler reappeared, approaching the car at a speed far exceeding his usual stately pace.

While Hilary opened the car and climbed out, Bateson said, his voice tremulous:

"If you please, miss, Doctor Kinross would like you to come upstairs at once—"

She followed him into the house where she was escorted across the great square hall with its minstrels' gallery, Jacobean oak chests and high-backed tapestried chairs, with paintings worth a fortune framed in heavy gilt against the oak wainscoting lining the wide, shallow staircase up which she climbed behind the butler's portly figure.

Then she was in a luxurious sitting-room furnished in turquoise, ivory and gold – a delicately feminine room which seemed an incongruous setting for the big, tweed-suited man who, his face grey with worry, paced up and down while Blake, quiet and self-possessed, was attempting to calm him.

"But she can't be operated on up here – she can't!" Fairfax was saying furiously. "She must have the best, if it's got to be done – the best surgeon and anaesthetist this country has—"

"Look," Blake pointed out patiently, "you're a Northerner yourself – I should have thought you'd surely have enough faith in the excellent medical men who live and work outside Harley or Wimpole Streets." He held up a hand as Fairfax would have burst forth again. "As it happens, you're very fortunate. Sir Keith Lowson is one of the best surgeons in Europe – ordinarily he would be in

Liverpool, but just now he happens to be in Windermere – staying at the Old England. I'll have a personal word with him, and I'm sure he'll be happy to come to our aid."

"Oh!" For a moment Fairfax looked taken aback. "Well, he'd certainly make me feel more comfortable. But what nursing home is good enough – and then there's the anaesthetist. I—" He looked shamefaced for a moment. "I've always had a horror of anaesthetics, and I don't mind admitting it! And Lena—" He broke off, and turned aside to stare out of the uncurtained window, his hands clenching and unclencing as he stared at the darkening line of the mountains against the twilit sky.

"You have no need to worry about either of those matters." Blake glanced across to where Hilary was standing silently just inside the doorway. "I'm going to try to contact Sir Keith right away. Hilary, will you get one of the servants to take you to another telephone, where I want you to put through a call to the usual nursing home in Windermere and tell them to prepare for a patient with a possible perforated appendix. The operation must take place at the earliest moment. But first of all, arrange for an ambulance to come immediately." He paused a moment and as she nodded and was about to leave the room, said sharply: "Wait, please. I'd better speak to Sir Keith, first – if he's available. Then you can tell the home whom to expect—"

He crossed to a small window in a table bay and picked up the telephone, swiftly dialling a number. After a brief pause during which Hilary looked with pity across at the big, white-faced man who stood watching the doctor intently, Blake spoke again:

"Sir Keith Lowson? Blake Kinross here – speaking from Tarndale. Good evening, sir. Sorry to interrupt your holiday like this, Sir Keith, but an emergency has arisen here – a patient of mine, Mrs. Vernon Fairfax. . . . I suspect a perforated appendix. Yes, as you say. . . . Certainly not a moment to be lost. . . . I was wondering if you could possibly see your way to. . . . Well, that's extremely kind of you. Mr. Fairfax is with me, and is naturally terribly worried. . . . He's saying he can never be grateful enough if you will. . . ." He gestured to Hilary, who nodded, and quietly leaving the room went along the corridor and to the head of the stairs, followed by Blake's voice: "Yes, that's the best nursing home in the town – I know the private wing of the hospital is packed to capacity. . . . We'll be there just as soon as the ambulance can make it. My secretary is already dealing with that—"

Hilary did not need to ask the butler, who was hovering anxiously in the hall, for the whereabouts of the telephone, for she had already seen one on a table at the foot of the staircase. Picking it up, she dialled, and in a very short time had arranged everything necessary with the head of the nursing home, and rang off with the information that an ambulance would be on its way in a matter of minutes; and that a bed would be prepared and the theatre ready for Sir Keith.

With quite astonishing swiftness a white ambulance was drawn up before the front door. It was Hilary who superintended the men carrying a stretcher under Blake's keen-eyed supervision. Lena, her beauty disfigured and contorted by sudden spasms of pain which even the injection Blake had given her earlier could not entirely alleviate, was lifted from her luxurious bed, and with gentle expertness carried downstairs and out to the waiting vehicle. With a little moan she put out a hand, and her husband, trembling himself, caught it strongly.

"It's all right, my darling – you'll soon be better," he comforted her huskily.

But she did not seem to see or hear him. Her eyes gazing wildly upward, stared for a moment into Blake's grave face. "Oh, it's you," she said drowsily, and then with another little cry: "Help me, Blake – help me—!"

"You're going to be all right," he said reassuringly, and glancing at Hilary. "Will you go with her? I'll follow in the car. Sir Keith will be there by the time you arrive."

"Very good," Hilary answered quietly, once more Nurse Talgarth; and as the ambulance men made their charge as comfortable as possible, she stepped in after them and the doors were shut.

"Well, thank heaven we were in the very nick of time. A few hours more, and Mrs. Fairfax would have been beyond saving with even the latest of our so-called miracle drugs."

Sir Keith Lowson, tall and distinguished-looking with grey hair sweeping back from a wide forehead, glanced across at his guests whom he had invited into his hotel suite for a late drink some hours later. With Blake assisting at the operation Hilary had determined to stay at the nursing home in case she should be needed. As it happened she was – for it was she who had persuaded Vernon Fairfax, after the operation was pronounced satisfactory, that his wife would be kept under the effects of the anaesthetic all through the hours of the night, and would not awaken before morning, to allow her to telephone to Charles the chauffeur to fetch him. The assurance that he would be able to speak with Lena as soon as she recovered consciousness the next morning at last made him give a reluctant consent to be taken back to his own home; and it was with considerable relief that they had at last got rid of the half distraught man whose cool ruthlessness, so suddenly shattered, had left him as defenceless as any ordinary mortal. Although this was not the time to allow such a thought to obtrude, Hilary could not avoid the feeling that Lena had hardly shown herself worthy of such a depth of devotion. But perhaps when she had fully recovered from the shock of this illness she would be different, Hilary thought with characteristic generosity.

152

"The little fool!" Sir Keith continued, as a waiter entered the sitting-room with more smoked salmon sandwiches and a further supply of champagne. "She must have had considerable bouts of pain over a long time – dosed herself with things to drown the attacks, I suppose! How often have I not experienced that type of prelude where these fashionable, pleasure-loving ladies are concerned. In one way it's lucky this particular case flared so quickly, for she's the type to work herself into hysteria at the prospect of nursing homes and operations. But as I say, she's darned lucky to be alive!"

"It's not going to be a quick business, is it, sir?" Blake observed. "All the poison will leave her weak for quite a time – so stupid, when a straightforward appendix patient recovers so quickly."

"Undoubtedly," Sir Keith agreed. "I'll have to stay and keep an eye on her for the next few days – that complication we found can leave nasty after-effects if we don't take care. Then once she's back home – no need to worry while she's here, for the nursing is excellent – you'll have to keep an eye for several weeks. She'll need two nurses when she first goes home – and I should think," he added rather drily, "another for that husband of hers! So often the same with these tough tycoons – go all to pieces in a medical emergency!"

"That's so," Hilary nodded. "I've seen those big tough men go to pieces before, but somehow I thought he wasn't the type, poor man."

"H'm! Easy to see that's a case of an older man being desperately in love with a younger wife – though that is a most unprofessional remark and is strictly *in camera*!" Sir Keith nodded shrewdly. He put down his glass and smiled across at them as they finished their drinks. "I'm getting on a bit myself, for this sort of emergency call. And it's only now that I remember I have to wish both you young people very great happiness. You're marrying the right sort of girl, Blake; and as for you, my dear," he shook his head, smiling at Hilary, "easy to see you're a born nurse! I heard something about your being at St. Winifred's and having to leave. Pity, if I may say so."

"Yes, alas." Quietly she explained how she had been forced to give up. "But I always cherished the hope that one day I should be allowed to take it up again. Only now—" impulsively she put out a hand to Blake, who took it in his own, "I've found another, even better job—"

They smiled at each other, and Sir Keith merely raised one eyebrow, which was comment enough; and on that note the belated little party broke up.

Motoring back to Tarnmere, Blake left his beloved at the gate of Willowbeck Farm, where a light in one window showed Cousin Priscilla was anxiously waiting up.

"Oh dear, she'll want to hear all about it – and I'm so tired," Hilary sighed. "Tomorrow the village will be humming with the news. I hope after this," she frowned a little, "that Vernon Fairfax will be suitably grateful to you. If you hadn't acted so quickly, he might have been a widower by now. There was bad peritonitis, wasn't there – and other complications. If Sir Keith feels he'll still have to keep an eye on her for a few days, that means it really was dangerous—"

"My love, you rate my part in the affair much too high," he told her, bending forward to kiss her above one winged eyebrow. "Certainly it was touch and go at one stage, and it was the luck of the lord that we had Sir Keith just where he was most wanted tonight. Goodnight, sweetheart, and thank you for all *you've* done. What a clever fellow I am, finding myself such a girl!"

She returned his last kiss, and then ran up the path, turning to wave as he drove off.

Cousin Priscilla was there, ready to see her into bed with a hot drink. It was obvious that Mrs. Brathay was

154

longing to ask questions she was nobly curbing, and while she undressed Hilary gave her cousin a brief resumé of what had happened.

"My word!" Cousin Priscilla shook her head. "What excitement for the village tomorrow. Those Fairfaxes have brought a deal of excitement to Tarnmere – but that's only to be expected when you get these millionaire sort of folk in a quiet place!"

"This is one bit of excitement we could all have done without!" Hilary returned with a yawn. "Most of all poor Lena herself. She's going to pay for her stupidity in letting that appendix flare like that. And I don't envy Blake or any of those who have to look after her, because if ever anyone has the making of a bad invalid, she will as soon as she's strong enough. And that's not being unkind, only realistic," she added sleepily.

"Happen you're reet, love," Mrs. Brathay returned in the vernacular, adding with a laugh as she went out of the room: "I've seen the lady, don't forget, and so I'm more than inclined to agree with you!"

Frant had to be included among those whose sympathy towards the patient was somewhat lukewarm. On hearing what had happened during the previous dramatic evening her comment was:

"Confound the woman! Now the portrait won't be finished for weeks. And it was getting on so well. Also, I wanted it out of the way. Of course, though I'm sorry she's ill – stupid creature, nearly killing herself like that – the sooner I'm done with the Fairfaxes and their house the better pleased I shall be."

"Well, she certainly won't be fit either in health or looks to sit for you for some time," Hilary warned.

"Blast! However, I suppose I can go ahead with the background the sitter is so keen to be shown against." Frant looked across the studio where Hilary had called on her way to the village. "Would you like to come up to the house and see it? I don't mind *you* looking at it, though I've issued a caveat that her husband is not to hang around until I'm further advanced."

Hilary hesitated. "I must confess I'd like to see it. But I feel rather as though I were trespassing—"

"Why on earth should you? She insisted on being painted in her own home instead of here; and the room there is entirely mine until the portrait is completed. I've even got a key to one of the garden doors, and have been positively commanded to come and go as I choose – all the servants know that; so if I want to take a friend along I have every right to," Frant replied. She had been looking cross, but as she glanced across at her friend, her attractive grin appeared. "Matter of fact, I'd like your opinion!"

This was an undoubted honour, and Hilary said: "In that case I'd like to come when you can spare the time."

"The present is as good as any. I don't mind telling you, I wouldn't let even John see anything but the finished work," Frant observed. "I suppose as it's Saturday morning your affianced won't be needing you at that wretched typewriter."

"No, he's over in Windermere attending upon Sir Keith. So is the husband – making a nuisance of himself, I expect, poor fellow," Hilary returned, following her friend out of the house.

"How long do they expect to keep her in?" Frant asked as they walked along the road which led to Hollins Hall.

Hilary shook her head. "Too early to say yet. I should think at least a fortnight to three weeks under the circumstances. Then it will be another month before she's anything like normal."

"Poor thing!" Frant sounded genuinely sympathetic. "But what do you bet she'll be pure hell when she's convalescent? It would take more than a burst appendix to alter that one's essential – I'm afraid I can only call it

156

bitchiness. Or do you believe in the softening effect of a shock like yesterday's?"

"I'm afraid not," Hilary agreed. "However, let's be charitable and hope for the best."

Frant grinned. "The realistic nurse overcoming your natural kindness, my dear. Here we are. Come in and tell me just how true a likeness this is going to be."

They had climbed a steep drive, and now, outside a glass-panelled garden door on the north side of the house, Hilary's companion produced a key and let them in.

The door led into a long passage, and nobody seemed about as Frant led the way and pausing, opened a door leading into a big room with a bright northern light that made it eminently suitable for painting. At one end, under a glass skylight in the roof, a gilt Louis Quinze chair upholstered in purple velvet stood on a sumptuous carpet, while behind it silken hangings of a paler blue than the velvet swept regally across long arched windows. The empty chair seemed to have something of the air of a vacant throne waiting for some being of incredible grandeur, wonderfully gowned and gleaming with jewels.

Seeing her friend's eyes widen a little, Frant gave her a sidelong smile.

"Terribly grand, isn't it?" she observed. "Which is, of course, what it's meant to be! Now!" She crossed to where a covered canvas stood on its easel facing that empty chair, and removed the white cloth drape.

At her first view of the unfinished portrait Hilary could only stare for long moments, bereft of comment.

"Well?" The artist's smile widened as she saw the appreciation not unmingled with shocked amusement in her first viewer's expression.

"Lord! You *have* been ruthless," Hilary commented. "Does she really like it?"

"I don't know. So far the only comment was: 'Does my mouth look just a little hard?' But she keeps on saying of course it isn't finished yet, and she's sure it'll be a sensation when it is."

"It will be!" Hilary agreed. "And you say Fairfax himself hasn't seen it?"

"I did allow him a glance the other day. *He's* no art critic, darling. But it's a status symbol to be painted by V. Frant – or so I gather." Lighting a cigarette, she surveyed her work through half-closed eyes. "But he's not the person who thinks so. What he wants is to see his beautiful wife on an expensive canvas next year at Burlington House. And if she sees anything she doesn't particularly like when I'm through, she'll never say so."

Hilary was silent, staring in fascination at the slender figure seated in that regal chair. Lena had chosen to be painted in a gown of unrelieved white velvet which was cut on almost mediaeval lines; the artful simplicity of which proclaimed – as Frant caustically commented *"Couture* at its most *haute!"*

The white of the dress stood out in colourful drama against the purple of the chair in which she was half turned towards the viewer, and when the paler purple of the silken hangings was finished, the result would certainly be startling enough to gather crowds at Burlington House.

But it was the face of the sitter which riveted attention first and foremost. All Lena's pride, selfishness and shallow acquisitiveness was subtly portrayed behind that vivid beauty. The skilfully painted mouth that hinted at passions not easily controlled, the contradictory coldness of those ice-blue eyes, a certain assured insolence in the pose.

Yes, thought Hilary, marvelling at her friend's ruthless penetration, there was beauty there – but beauty marred by the inward character of the sitter. Many people would see only the surface – the portrait of a beautiful woman. Viewers would comment on how striking a picture had been painted of the wealthy and lovely Mrs. Vernon Fairfax. Those who saw the essential flaws behind that beauty would be a discerning minority.

Hilary said: "Thank goodness Fairfax has seen and approved! It's lucky his business shrewdness didn't extend to what lies behind this!"

"Living with the original, I hardly thought he would do other than approve," Frant said drily. "By the way, ducky, forget this private view, please."

"Of course." Then Hilary's natural kindness asserted itself: "Oh dear! I *do* hope the shock of what's happened will improve her—"

"But you still doubt it. However. Let us be optimists." Frant covered the canvas again, before leading the way from the room and locking the door. "With Candide we can always hope for the best in this best of all possible worlds! And if that sounds as sarcastic as old Voltaire himself, who shall blame me?"

CHAPTER ELEVEN

LENA put down the book she had been listlessly trying to read, and raising herself among the silken cushions of the chaise-longue which had been drawn up before the long windows, looked disconsolately at the view beyond. The loveliness of gardens ablaze with roses and bordered by emerald turf, and the enchanting little island with its marble pavilion seeming to float on the mountain reflecting waters of the lake meant nothing to her. And yet when her husband had told her with evident delight that she would be well enough to travel in ten days or so, she had insisted that she wanted to stay where she was.

But she knew that soon – very soon – she would change her mind, and be glad of a change of scene. But this was the first beautifully sunny day after a week of mist and rain, and for once her spirits were somewhat lightened. Heaven knew the dark green of a Lakeland July had held little enough appeal, and as she thought back on the at first discomfort and then maddening boredom of convalescence in the month which had elapsed since that night when for a brief time her life had hung in the balance, she knew that there was only one thing and one thing only that kept her in Tarnmere. The fact that when she left here she would also be leaving the man who during these last weeks had been her daily visitor – Blake Kinross. Somehow she knew that, especially in these last two weeks, his presence had become at first imperceptibly and then more and more clearly, necessary to her feeling of wellbeing.

At first, when she began to get better in the nursing home, it had been different. There were so many people around that it had not been too bad, stitches and all.

160

Friends came from afar to visit her, dozens more had loaded her with flowers and gifts, and letters and telegrams; she had read of her indisposition in the gossip columns of the papers with a definite satisfaction. And dear Sir Keith Lowson, so distinguished and sympathetic, had been a flattering appendage to her illness. All the nursing staff were pleasantly fluttered by the great man, and they had been in constant attendance, making her revel in being a palely beautiful and interesting invalid.

But then after a fortnight she had been pronounced well enough to come home. At first with a nurse who after a week was, had Lena known it, quite as thankful to give up her increasingly difficult patient as the patient was to see her go. Now her own maid and the staff were enough to see to her comfort – and deal with her tantrums which increased with her strength!

But now, when Vernon wanted her to convalesce abroad, she found herself increasingly reluctant to exchange what was otherwise present boredom for travel and gaiety. And again the knowledge came to her that the cause, the one redeeming feature, was – her doctor. Somehow a great deal, if not all, the attraction she had once felt for Blake had returned with renewed force. And the knowledge that he was as far out of reach as the mythical man in the moon filled her hard, shallowy acquisitive mind with anger and frustration.

She knew that all the talk in the village was of "our doctor's" approaching marriage – so soon to take place now in the little church. What he could *see* in Hilary Talgarth passed her comprehension; but the knowledge of how much those two so evidently meant to each other filled her with venomous jealousy.

As for herself – she certainly could not rest under any deception that he ever treated her with anything but the most maddeningly distant courtesy. Of course as her medical man he couldn't possibly have done otherwise, even had he wished to show a warmer side to his character where she was concerned. But the knowledge that no intention could possibly have been further from his mind and heart – that heart which was so completely another girl's – wounded her pride to an extent she would not admit even to herself.

On top of this Vernon's constant anxious solicitude was beginning to bore and irritate her to screaming point. In one way it would be a relief to take his advice and get right away. And yet – and yet—

As the days passed she knew that she had found herself looking forward more and more eagerly to her old flame's visits. At first it had been easy to pretend what a dull stick the prospect of matrimony had turned him into. But from the first, as soon as she was well enough to be aware of him again, she knew how far from dull he was. His quiet presence, his disturbing good looks gave him a new, mature fascination that had been lacking in the very young man she had once known. Anyway, he was due this afternoon at any moment, and glancing across at her graceful reflection, her rapidly returning beauty aided by a well-known beauty specialist, up from London at enormous cost and staying at the White Lion, she felt a glow of self-satisfaction as she reclined on the day-bed.

Then the door opened after a discreet tap, and Angélique, her French maid, announced:

"Doctor Kinross, madame."

"Oh, here you are!" As Lena held out a welcoming hand, the girl withdrew circumspectly, but on the other side of the door permitted herself a knowing smile. Madame was bored, and had been apt to be even more unpleasant and exacting than usual during these last days. If the good doctor's visits (Ah, but he was *un joli type*, enough to make any feminine heart flutter) improved that one's temper, so much the better for those who had the

162

task of looking after her. Madame was bored with her surroundings, herself and most certainly her husband; the last being manifestly unfair when Monsieur had shown himself the perfect model of a devoted and anxious spouse. *Mais que voulez-vous?* It was the old, old story of the elder husband and the young wife desirous of flattery from younger and handsomer men! Angélique shrugged sardonically, but thought: "Madame had best have a care! There is a volcano of jealousy simmering in Monsieur. Once let it have cause to erupt and – pouf! all might lie in ruins!"

As having briefly shaken hands Blake said briskly, "You're looking very well. Time you had some exercise," she laughed.

"Oh, I'm the laziest woman on earth – don't you know that? Anyway, do ring for tea and have some while you scold me."

"Thanks, but I'm afraid that's not possible," he answered. "I've just looked in because I shall be away for the next few days."

"Oh, but why?" Her eyes widened in dismay.

"A medical conference," he replied briefly.

"But you'll come and see me as soon as you're back?"

"Quite unnecessary – I told you. You won't need a doctor, and I'm too busy to attend to cured patients."

"But, Blake, I get so miserably depressed!" she protested.

"Post-operational depression. It will wear off. Don't think about yourself so much," he said, and then gently: "Get back to your normal way of life – don't overdo things, of course. But a month in the South of France will put you right on your feet."

"So this is goodbye?" she said wistfully.

"*Au revoir*, anyway."

"It must be only that. I shall miss you horribly. You know," her voice broke, and there were sudden tears in her eyes (she had always found tears an easy way to soften her husband), "it's been rather wonderful, seeing so much of you again."

"Good lord! Why?"

"Well, perhaps I'm a fool, but however badly I behaved, I can't quite forget. Haven't you found out yet that I'm not *happy*?"

"You are, you know, when you don't dramatise yourself. Cheer up, Lena. And now I really must be off."

"No!" She caught his hand, holding it with unexpected strength. "My dear, I can't thank you enough for your care of me. If only—" she lowered her voice," you could care still – just a little—"

"Don't be silly –" he began, both angry and embarrassed as he looked at her, unconscious of those clinging fingers.

Neither of them had noticed the opening door, and for a moment Vernon Fairfax regarded the tableau in silence. Then as he spoke his wife's name sharply she gave a startled exclamation and dropped Blake's hand abruptly.

"Sorry if I'm interrupting," said Fairfax, and there was no mistaking the iron in his tone.

"Oh, Vernon, such good news! The doctor has just told me I can go to France as soon as – as we like—"

"I knew that already. In fact, when I said something of the same kind earlier, you didn't seem particularly enthusiastic." Even in her own ears Lena's would-be lightness had sounded false, and now as her husband advanced into the room, his glance at the doctor was hard and unfriendly. "I presume," he continued deliberately, "that my wife's recovery will mean that your visits will become – no longer necessary, Doctor Kinross?"

"I've just told Mrs. Fairfax so," said Blake.

There was a moment's uncomfortable silence. Blake's eyes held the other man's hostile stare, his own expression coolly withdrawn.

"Excellent!" Fairfax put undue emphasis into the one cold word.

When Blake took his leave, he received the curtest of nods from his patient's husband, a tremulous half-smile from the patient herself, and going down the corridor was frowning in considerable exasperation. Confound Lena and her theatrical gesture! Of course Fairfax had put the worst possible interpretation on what he had seen. Anyway, thank heaven he was done with this most unwelcome case!

Alone with Lena, Fairfax glanced down at his wife, his heavy brows drawn together in a frown.

"Do you usually hold hands with your doctor?" he observed rather harshly.

"Oh, don't be so stupid, Vernon. I was only thanking him." Lena had herself completely in hand again now. "How unfair and ungrateful you are! In fact you seem to forget if he hadn't acted so promptly I might not be here at all."

"I admit that," he answered drily. "But is that any reason for you to hold the fellow's hand?"

"Of course if you don't trust me – Oh, how dare you!" Those easy tears were there again.

"I'm sorry, Lena." He bent over and kissed her. "But I can't forget the past entirely. And women seem to have such a habit of overdoing their gratitude to their doctors!"

"I think that's rather insulting," she said coldly. "Please ring for tea." And she knew that as was so often the case she had already made him feel completely in the wrong. But while they talked of casual, everyday things, the scene apparently forgotten, her thoughts were darting like little arrows of venom through her mind:

"It's no use pretending I'm not going to miss Blake like hell . . . If only he hadn't got so terribly attractive . . . And if Vernon knew how ugly and how much older he looks when he scowls, he might try

165

to be pleasanter . . . I suppose by the time I see Blake again he'll be
married to that Talgarth girl . . . I do think life can be horribly
unfair!"

And while tea was served, round and round the thought
wheel of her shallow self-pity whirled; while the demon of
discontent grew steadily stronger in her self-centred heart.

Pausing before the steel file in her office, a folder of papers
in her hands, Hilary stared out at the brightness of the
herbaceous border opposite, her eyes dreamy.

Somehow it had become an increasing habit with her
lately: one which she had told her beloved was a quite
disgraceful habit of being engaged! For although Blake
had still wanted her to marry him very soon, it had been
finally decided that they should have a September wedding when the harvest was gathered in, and Tim and so
many of their friends would be able to make what the
village termed "a reet proper do" on the great day. In this
Cousin Priscilla concurred; for not only did it give her
plenty of time to make preparations, but she was also able
to indulge in her invariable custom of visiting her sister in
Scotland, stating that she liked Tarnmere least of all in
August when it was crawling with visitors and, far worse,
day trippers who literally clogged up and littered the
landscape. So both Hilary and Blake had agreed that it
would be nicer all round when the majority of holidaymakers had gone and Tarnmere was once more beginning to
revert to its peaceful self. At present, with cafés and hotels
packed to overflowing, shouting loads of boat-rowers from
the landing stage run by a man who had managed to
establish his business in the teeth of ferocious opposition, it
would not have been Hilary's idea of an ideal wedding with
crowds of gaping strangers flashing cameras and getting in
the way of their own friends and relations.

Anyway, Hilary decided, it was heaven to be engaged;
heaven to look forward to the day when she would belong

166

to Blake completely— For two days she had had to do without Blake, but now he was back.

"Dreaming, beloved?" His voice just behind her made her turn with a start, nearly dropping the folder she held.

"Yes." She raised her face for his kiss. "A disgraceful lapse on the part of your secretary, Doctor Kinross. She deserves the sack!"

"She's going to get it very soon – in exchange for a lifetime job that she won't find always very easy," he said, his lips close to hers.

"Oh, are you trying to frighten me?" She put up a hand, stroking his cheek. "I warn you, I'm not easily scared!"

"You don't need to tell me that, my sweet! What have you got there?" He glanced at the folder and seeing the name on it, frowned. "H'm! The Fairfax dossier. Put it away, for goodness' sake. Thanks be, she's completely cured – though she doesn't want to believe it, and I must confess to being tired of of being glowered at by that idiot husband of hers. He should realise that I couldn't be less interested in his spoiled empty-headed wife than if she were the Witch of Endor!"

Hilary laughed, shaking her head at him. "An unkind comparison – yet I have an idea Mrs. Fairfax is inclined to call up, not spirits but memories from the past – memories that probably flatter her ego! It's your fault for being so attractive, you know, Doctor Kinross!"

"Don't talk so daft!" he admonished, reddening.

Hilary cocked a knowing eye at him. "Do you tell me the female-falling-for-her-physician syndrome didn't work at all? I bet it did. But I think she's learned to be wary of that jealous husband of hers."

"She will if she knows what's good for her," he returned rather grimly. "Let's forget 'em both, anyway. What about a run up to Keswick and a spot of dinner this evening?"

"Darling, I'd love to, but I've promised to help poor

Tim with his accounts – he's such a rotten adder-up and he's in the most awful mess. Also, I think we're in for yet another storm – I do wish August wasn't so thundery."

"Maybe you're right," he agreed, looking out to where an ominous line of black cloud loomed over the peaks across the valley. "Spoil the fun in the seven-acre field if it thunders! But you tell Tim from me it's time he got a wife of his own with a good head for figures, as he's not going to have his helpful sister to lean on much longer!"

She laughed. "Tim will be much more concerned with his wife's figure than any possible head she may have for figures!" she observed with sisterly frankness.

"Well, if you're heartlessly going to leave me alone, you might at least kiss me again before you go," said Blake. A suggestion which met with willing response!

After his beloved left him Blake dined alone, aware of a slightly disconsolate feeling. He settled down with a book until eleven o'clock when he decided to go to bed. He was on his way upstairs when the telephone began to ring.

Going back, he reached for the instrument with a grunt. *Now* what? But at the voice that came across the wire, choked and on a note of near hysteria, his fingers tightened about the telephone and he frowned.

"Is Doctor Kinross there – it's urgent!" Then: "Oh, Blake, I'm feeling so desperately ill. Please come at once—"

His mouth tightening in repressed exasperation, he said: "What's the matter? You were quite all right when I last saw you—"

"But I'm not all right now – I'm feeling dreadful, and I'm really in pain." Again there was that note of rising hysteria. "And Vernon's away, old Bateson's on holiday, and I've given the rest of the staff, including my maid, the evening off to go to that wretched circus they're holding somewhere near Ambleside. I've got the most awful pain in my side, and I'm so frightened—"

There was only one answer to such an appeal. "Very well," he agreed curtly, "I'll come along. Have you been eating anything that can have disagreed with you?"

"Not a thing. Oh, please, please come quickly!" The line clicked dead and for a moment Blake stared frowningly into the telephone. Never had he felt more reluctant to answer a call for his help.

A few minutes later he guided the car out of the garage and was driving along the pitch dark road, lit by occasional vivid flashes of lightning, while a growling mutter of thunder told of a storm in one of the adjoining valleys.

When he arrived at Hollins Hall ten minutes later the windows of Lena's apartments were shining out, the curtains undrawn. For a moment he wondered how on earth, if all the servants were out, he was going to get in. Then he saw a big envelope lying near the front door, and picking it up, realised she must have thrown down a key from her bedroom window.

As he turned the big key in the lock the great door opened to show the vast, dimly lit hall. Knowing his way about, he mounted the stairs, his face rather set, and making his way along the all too familiar corridor, knocked at the door of Lena's sitting-room, but received no response. His frown deepening, he did the same to her bedroom door, and this time was greeted by a faint "Come in—"

Entering, he closed the door behind him, and looking across saw her sitting in a chair near the flower-filled fireplace. She was in a becoming apricot-coloured negligée which he was in no mood to appreciate; and though she was pale she was not so ill that she had omitted a most becoming though invalidish make-up.

"Thank goodness you've come!" She made a movement as though to rise, and then with a little cry sank gracefully back, pressing a hand to her side. "Oh – !"

"Now what's all this?" he demanded, going across to

169

her. "Why did you give your maid an evening off if you weren't feeling well, for heaven's sake?"

"But I was all right earlier," she said plaintively. "In fact, at tea-time I was fine. Veronica Frant came to tea to discuss when we should resume the final sittings for my portrait. It was only after she had gone that I felt a little queasy and just a faint pain. But it passed off, and I let Angélique go out with the others – in fact, I rather enjoyed the idea of an evening to myself and just the TV. Then – about an hour and a half ago – I began to feel really ill."

"Have you been sick?" he demanded sharply, taking out his stethoscope.

"No, but I've felt – deadly." She raised a hand to her forehead, closing her eyes. "And for the last week I've kept on getting these awful waves of misery – just feeling as though I could throw myself out of the window—"

"That's nothing but post-operative depression in its later stages – I've already warned you about it." His tone was crisp while he took her pulse and then listened to her heart. "You did quite wrong to let yourself be left alone in this house, in your present state of nerves."

"How right you are," she said faintly. "And then there's been thunder about – and thunder always terrifies me. Oh, I hope I'm not going to be really ill again."

"Certainly you're not." He finished his examination, the slight frown between his brows deepening. "There's nothing whatever wrong with you except nervous depression. I'll fix you a sedative and leave you some pills to take in half an hour when you will, if you take my advice, get to bed and try to relax."

Blake went across to a table by the window on which he had placed his bag and selected some pills from the numerous bottles within. A sob sounded behind him, and when he glanced round he saw, with some exasperation, that she had dissolved into a storm of tears.

"Do try to control yourself!" he ordered more sharply

than was usual with him. He crossed to the luxuriously fitted wasbasin and pouring some water from the tap into a tumbler shook some grains into it. "Here, take this."

She accepted the glass, swallowed the contents, and then with a cry let the tumbler fall on the rose and turquoise Chinese carpet, getting to her feet in a swift movement and throwing her arms about his neck.

"Blake, please try to understand – don't look at me in that – oh, that inhuman way!" she sobbed. "I'm so unhappy! I only want a little sympathy. If you knew what my life was like – tied to a jealous, stupid man who thinks he's bought me with his money! Meeting you again, seeing you as I have done, has made me realise the fool I was, even to think I could live without you—"

"Lena, for heaven's sake pull yourself together!" he commanded almost roughly, pulling her hands from about his neck. "This is nothing but hysteria which you can perfectly well control." And as she continued to sob hysterically: "Can't you see how selfishly ungrateful you're being? You chose Fairfax because you knew he could give you the sort of life you wanted. Well, you've had that life and will continue to have it, unless you make more of a fool of yourself than usual! But because you want to have your cake and eat it, you consider yourself ill done by – heaven knows why. Fairfax is devoted to you – far more than you deserve, and you have no right to have called me out at this hour and under these circumstances."

"I had to see you."

"There wasn't the least need. You weren't ill."

"Blake, I had to see you," she repeated. "Don't you understand? I love you—"

"For heaven's sake, what's all this rubbish?" Blake demanded. "You're crazy, Lena."

"I know I am – about you!" she told him passionately. "Oh, darling, be kind to me—" Again she was clinging to him desperately, determined to force response from this cold, contemptuous man. "You don't understand!" she cried.

He understood only too well. Here was the frustration of a sexy, self-centred woman. As for love – that was the last thing of which she was capable. But with appalling clarity he also understood his own situation, and what could come of it.

"Listen," he said, "from now on you must find another doctor, Lena. This is my final goodbye."

"But you loved me – once—"

"Not really." He was too angry to choose his words. "You attracted the kind of emotion which never lasts. The best thing you ever did was to show me what a young fool I'd been."

With startled, angry realisation of the cold contempt in his tone that was suddenly like a whiplash across her self-esteem, she stared up at him as he continued bitingly:

"I hope when you come to your senses you'll realise what a little fool you are. And that's all I have to say to you."

Turning on his heel, he snatched up his case and strode out of the room, leaving her to stare after him, her hands clenching and unclenching, her breast heaving with a very different emotion from her late induced attack of hysteria, her eyes suddenly hard and furious. But she was left, for once in her life, without a word to say.

And Blake, such blazing anger in possession that he could hardly see before him, his eyes hard, his mouth tight with anger, went swiftly down the passage towards the top of the stairs. Then as he reached them he stopped dead, staring unbelievingly at the man who stood at the top of the long flight, his face white with rage.

"So this is what I find when I come back unexpectedly!" Vernon Fairfax's voice was hardly raised, but molten as the reddened rage in his grey eyes. "If you must

172

have my wife with her arms about you at this hour of night, Kinross, you might at least have the wisdom to draw the curtains of her bedroom window! Or did you forget how easily you could be seen – ?"

Hearing voices, Lena opened her door, and seeing her husband, emitted a scream of genuine fear.

Fairfax looked past Blake, and said in a snarl: "Get back into your room – I'll have something to say to you in a minute!" And then, his eyes blazing into Blake's: "My God, Kinross! I've suspected something between you and my wife, ever since you were so assiduous in attending her long after you needed to. But she's well enough now – as any other doctor will testify. I should have thought," he laughed bitingly, "that you'd have had more sense of self-preservation than to visit her on a night when it's been arranged for some time past that the servants would all be out. But then of course you knew I was away—"

"Look here," Blake commanded, "your wife telephoned me to say she was taken suddenly ill. I don't expect you to believe that, but it's the truth. She's in a state of post-operative hysteria aggravated by her usual self-centred egotism! Considering that she's aware of my engagement to Hilary Talgarth, I consider her behaviour entirely unforgivable. The fact that she threw herself at me while I was preparing her a sedative is merely part and parcel of her absurd behaviour which—"

"I should hardly think you expect me to be fool enough to believe!" Fairfax's laugh was a bitter sneer. "I should also have thought you might have been man enough not to try to throw all the blame on my wife – fool though she is. But I'll see the blame lies squarely where it should lie, Kinross. As a doctor you know the penalty for 'unprofessional conduct' as your superiors term it. Well, I'll see they have a formal complaint laid against you – the whole damned B.M.A. I'll break you, Kinross, as I've broken better men before you."

"I don't think there's anything to be gained by this sort of melodrama," Blake returned coldly. "I realise how incriminating it must seem to you, but I swear most solemnly that I'm telling the truth. And believe me, whatever you try to do to me, the truth will prevail in the end."

"I've no doubt it will," Fairfax retorted savagely. "And 'the truth, the whole truth and nothing but the truth' will finish your career, both here and anywhere else you like to hide your rotten self. You'll be struck off, Kinross, and it's no more than you deserve. And now get out of my house!"

Blake looked at him, his face white with the angry helplessness that had him in its grip. What use to attempt further argument with this furious, jealous, half demented man?

Even if it were his word against Lena's husband's; even with the fact that there were no witnesses besides Fairfax himself, who had seen, with such damning clarity, Lena with her arms about Blake's neck, what hope could there ever be of proving the true reality of the situation? The mere accusation, the smear and suspicion it would leave, would be more than enough to lay his career in ruins.

Quietly he turned and went down the stairs; and as he passed through the door to his car, Vernon Fairfax's harsh, angry laughter was echoing in his ears.

CHAPTER TWELVE

"But, Blake, what are we to do? Vernon Fairfax can ruin you— Oh, I could kill that selfish beast of a wife of his!" Hilary faced her beloved, her face deathly white in the light of the following morning. "Supposing I go and see him – tell him how I believe in you, that he's making the most terrible mistake—"

"My darling!" Blake's voice was weary, his own face drawn. "It would be no use. Look how damning the whole wretched situation appears! Even if there's no proof from other witnesses, mud sticks. A formal complaint to the B.M.A. will be the end of me here."

He turned away, his mouth twisting. "A fine prospect for you! A husband with a smirched reputation, a doctor whom people will always point to and say 'No smoke without fire', or 'He shouldn't have been fool enough to be taken in – if he *was* taken in'. Can't you imagine it all?"

"Stop!" she commanded passionately. "It *shan't* be – it mustn't be, somehow we've got to prove the truth. Didn't Mrs. Tyson hear you take that telephone call?" She looked at him in sudden hope.

He shook his head unhappily. "No; she was in bed. I've simply no witnesses at all, my sweet. That's the utterly damnable part of it."

Hilary paced the room, her hands clenched, her eyes fierce and determined. "You shall be cleared – you must be!" she exclaimed. "I'll see Lena, force the truth from her—"

"And even if you did – if you persuaded her to acknowledge that fit of hysteria, she'd never make her husband

175

believe it," he returned. "No, my darling, we're in the worst mess we possibly could be in – and I simply don't see any way out."

She caught her breath on a sob, going to him and putting her arms about him.

"It's – so wickedly unfair. I—"

Then her tears were salt against his lips. "So long as you believe in me, there's something left. Though it's unfair not to release you at once—"

"Blake! Are *you* out of your mind?" she demanded. And then: "Wait! I believe Vernon Fairfax – rather likes me in his odd way. Maybe when he's cooled down I can see him and try to make him realise what a fool he's being. At least he might be easier to deal with than that selfish cat of a wife of his." Sudden hope dawned in her eyes as she looked up at him.

But Blake shook his head as Vernon Fairfax's voice came echoing back to him:

"I'll break you, Kinross – as I've broken better men before you!"

There spoke the man of property and power; who had, no doubt, broken many in his time; and would be most relentless of all to the man he considered had betrayed his trust.

The days seemed to pass on leaden hours, the most miserable of Hilary's life.

What to do – whether to try to see Fairfax and plead with him? What was the use when even now he might have written the fatal letter which could bring down Blake's career in ruins?

Confiding in the one friend she could trust, she took some comfort from Frant's sympathy and anger, but even Frant could not suggest any way out of the appalling impasse.

"The man's not normal, neither is that confounded girl," she said furiously. "Anyway, I'll never finish her blasted portrait – but a fat lot of help that will be." She

176

frowned out of the long windows of her studio where the two girls had been talking for over an hour.

"I dread the news leaking out – being all over the village at any moment," Hilary sat, twisting a handkerchief between her restless fingers. "The fact that nearly everyone would take Blake's part wouldn't prevent the most appalling scandal. Oh, Frant, why should this have happened when we were so happy?"

Impulsively Frant went across and put an arm round her. "Ducky, something must happen to make that fool Fairfax believe the truth. . . . Oh, hang the thunder, as if things weren't bad enough, we're in for another heck of a storm."

The weather had been brooding all day, the sky leaden above the mountain peaks. Now a crack of thunder right overhead proclaimed one of those Lakeland storms that can last for hours, and vivid lightning zig-zagged down from the mountain tops and along the stone walls where frightened sheep and cattle huddled from the blast of hot wind that suddenly went through the valley with a banshee-like howl.

"Heaven help any campers or anyone mad enough to be climbing in this!" Frant observed, hoping to take her friend's mind momentarily off her own misery. "You'd never guess from this murk that it's only three o'clock – the rain seems to be laying on something special even for these parts, doesn't it. . . . Hullo, what on earth are you doing here, John?"

Both girls looked round to see John Dallam's huge figure standing in the doorway. As always, he looked even bigger in streaming oilskins. They stared in surprise at his grim face, and he said, with unusual sharpness in his pleasant voice:

"Frant, I left that alpenstock with you the other day. I want it – and not a second's delay. There's an injured man been sighted lying on the upper slopes of Haredale Peak –

damned fool attempting to climb that of all mountains in this sort of weather – and a general warning's gone out to the rescue team. Blake's with us, and we're going up to get down whatever fool is lying there—"

"Good heavens!" Personal problems for the moment forgotten, both girls exchanged startled glances, and while Frant went quickly over to a cupboard and took out the required alpenstock she asked:

"Has anyone the faintest idea who could have been mad enough to even think of climbing Haredale Peak on a day like this?"

"Well, no one's sure, but there's a very good chance that it could be, of all idiots, Vernon Fairfax." John sounded even more grim. "No one else has been reported missing, but apparently he left his house quite early this morning – it was fine enough then, remember – saying he was going up there. He must be daft at his age!"

The girls exchanged startled looks. John knew nothing of what had happened at Hollins Hall, but it was easy enough to guess that Vernon Fairfax could have decided to work off his anger and misery in a way natural to a man of his tough temperament.

"Oh, John, do take care!" For once startled out of her flippant carelessness, Frant clung to his arm for a moment, and bending, he kissed her swiftly.

"Not to worry," he said rather roughly. "We're all experienced climbers. And whoever it is, we've got to get the poor devil down."

Hilary had already run past him, and in the murk of the storm found Blake standing beside a land-rover containing the entire rescue team, with the local police sergeant, another expert climber, at the wheel.

"Blake!" It was all she could do to prevent herself from running to him, but under the eyes of the other men she could only say: "Could it really be – Vernon Fairfax?"

"Well, he seems the likeliest idiot to attempt the climb,

178

on a day that threatened storms. On the other hand, it may be someone quite different. But whoever it is, he obviously can't be left there!"

He spoke with the same studied lightness that John was talking to Frant. "But don't worry – we'll bring him down safely." Leaning forward, he planted a swift kiss on her lips, and then he and John climbed into the land-rover which in a few moments was being driven swiftly along the rough track leading to the base of the mountain.

Standing side by side, the two girls watched it disappear. Neither spoke of the dread in their hearts. This was too great a crisis for speculation or the voicing of useless fears. They knew that here was something as old as time: the raging elements, the stark courage of the men going to brave that peak in some of the worst possible circumstances; and the possibility that neither might ever see the man of her heart again.

Haredale Peak – so called, some said, after the fact that the big mountain hares had made their homes on its lower slopes for longer than man could remember – was perilous on its lower slopes, with loose scree and treacherous rock falls even in fine weather; and on the higher slopes part consisted of an almost sheer wall that had tested the courage and skill of many seasoned climbers. Over the century it had taken a toll of lives that ran into three figures; and even when the sun shone out of a clear sky the topmost peaks had a cruel and forbidding look in their jagged loneliness.

The party, roped together started off, their heads bent against a howling wind. Thunder crashed overhead with increasing violence, and the slopes ahead and valley below were pierced by constant blinding flashes of lightning. But each member of the rescue party knew his job, and climbed steadily higher with calculated skill. The knowledge that a slip might mean not only one's own death but that of all one's comrades was something to be resolutely pushed to the back of the mind. Luckily, every member of the team had been born and bred among the mountains, and all had experienced this sort of ordeal before – though seldom in worse weather or under such perilous conditions.

The driving rain made already treacherous scree, that loose rock and stone ready to create a miniature avalanche at the unguarded placing of a mountain boot, an increasing menace. Then there were smooth surfaces where no alpenstock was of more than the slightest avail; as they climbed higher, only a cool eye, bare hands and gritted teeth took them up ledge by ledge, with the lower slopes a terrifying fall into eternity that had to be banished from the imagination. . . .

It was Police Sergeant Garthwaite, burly, cool-headed and imperturbable, who gained first sight of their quarry, and gave a signal which sent an answering thrill through each of his roped companions.

And then they were on a mercifully fairly broad ledge, and Blake, bending over the recumbent figure of the man who lay there with a broken leg and arm, kept conscious by the driving, icy rain.

For a moment Vernon Fairfax stared up into the face of the man he had threatened to ruin. Then the ghost of a sardonic smile passed over his white features.

"You, eh?" Bending his head, Blake could just hear the faint words above a momentary lull in the storm. "This comes of – losing one's temper. But they say – there's no fool like an old fool. I—" His eyes closed, and a moment later Blake, having delved into his pack, was giving the unconscious man an injection.

Then he glanced round, seeing John and Sergeant Garthwaite beside him, the four other men coming up from below.

"Stretcher – he's got to be roped. Then he'll do," he

180

said briefly; and the others set about obeying his orders.

Frant had got out her small car and driven Hilary to the foot of the mountain. They were comforted by the presence of Tim, who had been absent on farm business at Kendal Market, and in any case had never been a mountaineer. He said again and again, seeing the tragic strain in his sister's eyes:

"It'll be all right – of course it will. They're all experts and know just what they're about. Look, I'll go back to Willowbeck and bring the estate car. It – may be a help when they get down."

"That's a good idea. Bless you." Frant spoke with a travesty of her usual lightness, her hands holding powerful fieldglasses, which in the general murk were of no avail, not quite steady. Then as Tim strode off through the driving rain: "They're an awful long time, aren't they? I do wish one could see something of what's happening."

"They've only been gone an hour." Hilary glanced at her wrist-watch. "It just seems so much longer."

"It certainly does," her friend agreed, and huddling together beneath the somewhat inadequate shelter of an overhanging rock they waited – in this battle between brave men and the combined cruelty of storm and jagged mountain, the woman's part. It was an ordeal each knew they would never forget. With above all the haunting dread: would it end in triumph – or tragedy?

It was Hilary who, nearly two hours later, first spotted tiny figures above, in the clearing light of after-storm. The thunder had died away to a distant rumble, and the lightning came fitfully and seldom. She grasped Frant's arm, pointing upwards with a hand that trembled.

"They're bringing someone down – on a stretcher. Look, up away to the right. Not so very far away."

Frant raised her powerful glasses, and let out her breath in a long sigh.

"Thank God!" The words were as much a prayer as an exclamation. Then they turned, to see Tim driving at a reckless speed along the rough track.

Climbing out, he almost snatched Frant's glasses. Then: "By George, they've done it!" he exclaimed exultantly. "Whoever it is, they've got him down to safety. And that's a job I wouldn't care to do, and I don't mind owning to it!"

Hilary could not speak. She could only close her eyes, fight off the faintness which threatened, and then open her eyes again, fixing them on those ever-nearing figures.

After what seemed an unending age but was in reality only half an hour, the rescue team stood beside Tim's estate car, and the stretcher bearing Vernon Fairfax's unconscious body, placed gently inside.

"Safe at last!" Blake was beside his beloved, and his eyes in the white strain of his face spoke more than any words. "He must be got to hospital instantly. There's a leg and an arm to be set, and we shall have the effects of exposure to deal with. But he's lucky to get off so lightly."

"Aye. It was a reet difficult job," said Police Sergeant Garthwaite with cheerful understatement. "Anyhow, it's nice to be down out o' the cold!"

"It is indeed." Blake brought out a silver flask of brandy, and everyone took a generous swig – tactfully not noticing that the usually calm and collected Miss Veronica Frant was clinging convulsively to John Dallam's arm. It was once again a case of eyes saying far more than any words; but Hilary, breathless with her own joy and relief, felt a further warm satisfaction as she looked across at her best friend and her best friend's large young man. This time there was no mistaking the depth of the other girl's shaken heart; and Hilary was more than certain that John was at last to attain his own heart's desire.

Then, her nurse's training asserting itself, she followed her own beloved into the estate car; and with his hand clasped strongly in hers, was driven off by Tim on the eight-mile drive to the hospital.

CHAPTER THIRTEEN

"I WONDER if Mrs. Vernon Fairfax will derive any lasting benefit from the shock of her selfish life?"

"Heaven knows – and I'm afraid one couldn't care less," Hilary replied. "I do *wish* we didn't have to go to see her husband this afternoon, darling. It will be most uncomfortable."

"I agree. Particularly as I shall always feel, in spite of Lena's confession, he'll have a sneaking feeling I may have still been keen on his wretched wife." Blake's tone was grim. "Still, thank heaven Lena won't be there. She's managed one visit, and is now 'under sedation in her own room at home'. To which Doctor Earlham from Windermere is more than welcome to attend!"

"I simply wouldn't have agreed to come if Frant hadn't told me, for some extraordinary reason, that we must accept the invitation," Hilary went on. "When I asked why on earth we should, she would only chuckle mysteriously – which is most unlike her – and say: 'You've got to go. You're in for a surprise, ducky'."

Blake turned to look at his love, an eyebrow raised. "What on earth has Frant got to do with this? I thought she had no other thoughts but for her engagement to young John."

"So had I. Thank goodness she's made up her mind at last that John *will* be a suitable wife for an artist! He'll always dote on her and I know they're going to be terribly happy." Hilary gave an ecstatic sigh, but a moment later her smile faded. "I'll be so glad when this visit is over. What can Vernon Fairfax want with us so urgently? And how in the name of goodness can Frant know anything about it? If she knows something, she might at least have told me."

"I couldn't agree more. However, here we are, so I suppose we'll soon know what it's all in aid of." Blake guided the car into the laurel-lined drive of the nursing home, and a few minutes later they were being shown into Vernon Fairfax's private ward.

He looked very pale, and much older propped up among his pillows, one leg in a formidable sling hanging from the ceiling. His greeting was strained, but they hardly noticed it in their surprise at the slim dark figure seated beside the bed. Fairfax indicated her with a wave of his sound hand.

"I can't pretended that I'm going to enjoy this," he said, "but Miss Frant here has been the means of showing me just what sort of a fool I have made of myself, and so," he gave a rueful, not unattractive smile, "the sooner we get it over the better. Over to you, Miss Frant."

"I feel rather a brute when this poor chap is still such an invalid," Frant observed, "but I do feel that this is something to be kept between the four of us and then forgotten. As I'm sure you will agree."

Blake raised his brows in silent surprise, and Hilary asked blankly:

"Frant, what *are* you talking about? And what on earth are you doing here?"

"I shouldn't be here," Frant told her, "if I hadn't visited Mrs. Fairfax on the evening of her – let's say, foolishness. We were discussing when the sittings for her portrait should be resumed, and when I left after having tea with her, I quite forgot that I'd been carrying a belonging of John's, which I left down beside my chair. I clean forgot about it, and it seems that after I left, no one noticed it left down by the chair I'd been sitting in. And evidently it fell over, opened and started itself—"

"But what –" Hilary began, and then stared in amazement as Frant bent down and picked up a square box which, on being opened, proved to be a tape-recorder.

"This is just one of those things," she said. "A chance in a million, one might say, or even the workings of Providence. Whatever it is, the machine started itself, and as it runs for ages, it very luckily picked up – this! Listen carefully."

She touched a switch, and Vernon Fairfax winced visibly as his wife's high, hysterical tones sounded through the room:

. . . *"I've had everything a girl could desire except real happiness."*

And then uncannily, Blake's voice, harsh and uncompromising:

"Lena, for heaven's sake, pull yourself together . . . This is nothing but hysteria which you can perfectly well control . . . Your main trouble is sheer, shallow selfishness . . . Vernon Fairfax is a decent fellow, who deserves better than that you should behave in this rotten way. I hope you'll realise what a little fool you are. And that's all I have to say to you."

Frant switched off the tape, and looked with compassion at the white-faced man on the bed. "I'm sorry to have had to put you through that again," she said. "But you agreed to it. And now I'll erase the whole thing, and you'll be sensible enough to forgive your wife for her stupidity."

"I'll try to forgive – though I doubt if I shall ever forget." There was weary bitterness in the older man's voice. "She swears she's learnt her lesson, that she didn't mean it at all – that she was lonely and it was part of the effect of her illness—" He looked at Blake, a mirthless smile hovering on his lips. "Are *you* ready to comfort an invalid with that assurance?"

"Most certainly I am." Blake took the hand held out to him, his warm smile reflected in his eyes. "I'm sorry you should have had to hear that—"

"I'm not." Fairfax turned his head wearily on the pil-

186

lows. "But at least I'm grateful to know how mistaken I was." He looked at Hilary. "I expect you find it – pretty difficult to forgive me?"

"Not in the least," she assured him, taking his hand in her turn. "Try to forget – and remove her from Tarnmere, anyway for a long time. She's been bored, and that's apt to make any woman behave stupidly."

"You're very kind. And I hope you'll both be as happy as you deserve." He looked at Blake, his hard eyes softening. "I've learnt that there are some things money can never entirely buy – but I'll try to forget this particular thing. I'll be more – realistic in future. This is where we say goodbye – and good luck."

It was a silent party that motored back to Tarnmere. Hilary said:

"That was – rather drastic of you, Frant. But we owe you our thanks, and it's lovely to know that you and John are going to do the sensible thing at last."

Frant observed: "I felt I couldn't do anything else. Fairfax needed to know the truth. He'll get over it – he's that sort. And I think his rather horrible Lena will have had enough of a fright to mend her ways."

Blake looked at her with a smile. "You don't mean to tell me you played that tape to Lena?"

Frant's laugh was grim. "I did. And the shock will do her good in the long run, though she's taking tranquillisers at the moment."

Hilary shook her head at her friend. "You're as drastic as your portrait painting, Frant dear. I don't know that I'm not a bit scared of you!"

Her friend grinned at her. "Maybe marriage to John will have a softening effect – though not on my work. I've told him, one mushy picture, and it's divorce! But he's a brave lad, and he says he's willing to take the risk."

"Well, our thanks to you, Frant, and now we'd better forget all about this afternoon," Blake observed.

"Certainly," Frant returned. "Drop me off at this corner, will you? I'll dot along to the studio and my young man."

They watched her slight, dark figure moving gracefully along the road, and then turned in at Blake's house.

There, alone in the sitting-room, he took her in his arms. "All's well that ends well after a very nasty interlude." He kissed her hard on her lips, and then, his cheek against her hair: "Nannie Tyson was right!"

"How?" She looked up at him enquiringly.

"She said that when the young woman crossed my path again: 'Mark my words, Master Blake, that one will bring you nothing but trouble!' Which proved only too true. But now we can finally forget her and concentrate on the fact that in a fortnight you'll be the local doctor's wife! Do you still feel you can bear the prospect, my love?"

"I adore the prospect!" she told him, raising her lips to his. "The unexpected telephone calls just when we don't want them, meals getting cold, people being a nuisance, people in need of real help – it will all be heaven, loving you as I do!"

"Complete heaven!" he agreed, his own lips once more against her own.

Doctor Nurse Romances

Don't miss
January's
other story of love and romance amid the pressure
and emotion of medical life.

TENDER LOVING CARE
by Kerry Mitchell

Stephanie loved nursing at the little Australian
country hospital, but why had Doctor Blair
Tremayne suddenly turned against her?

Order your copy today from your local paperback retailer.

189

Doctor Nurse Romances

and February's
stories of romantic relationships behind the scenes
of modern medical life are:

NURSE ON WARD NINE
by Lisa Cooper

It was a wrench for Claire Melville to leave home —
and Martin — to nurse at the Princess Beatrice Hospital,
and on Ward Nine she encountered hazards she had
never expected — not least that cold-eyed, moody
Doctor Andrew MacFarlane!

SATURDAY'S CHILD
by Betty Neels

Saturday's child works hard for a living . . . . And so
did Nurse Abigail Trent, plain and impoverished and
without hope of finding a husband. Why did she have
to fall in love with Professor Dominic van Wijkelen,
who hated all women and Abigail in particular?

Order your copies today from your local paperback retailer

Doctor Nurse Romances

Have you enjoyed these recent titles in our
Doctor Nurse series?

A ROSE FOR THE SURGEON
by Lisa Cooper

Was it Doctor Rob Delaney, who had once broken
Sister Anna's heart, who had sent her red roses? And
if not, who had?

THE DOCTOR'S CHOICE
by Hilary Wilde

Nurse Claire Butler had been brutally jilted. How
could she trust any other man — let alone the one
who had warned her not to fall in love on the rebound?

Order your copies today from your local paperback retailer.